The Magician

DEREK DWYER

First published 2006 through Lulu, Inc

(www.lulu.com/uk)

ISBN 978-1-4116-9262-6

This book is a work of fiction. The characters portrayed do not exist and any resemblance to persons alive or dead is entirely coincidental.

To Mary

Chapter1

The star liner Gigantean, 50,000 tonne flagship of the Yellow Star fleet, had been launched only weeks before from the New Caledonia shipyards in Orion's Belt and was crewed by the finest and most experienced officers in the Merchant Space Navy. Now she wallowed dead in space, like a burned-out booster from one of the antique chemical rockets that had ushered in the age of space exploration a thousand years ago.

As yet, none of the passengers and only a few of the crew were aware that there was a problem, but jury-rigged repairs were already being made and a full investigation had been begun. Some very difficult questions would have to be answered.

What unprecedented combination of circumstances could cripple the most sophisticated craft presently plying the space lanes? How did the designed-in multiple redundancy of all major components fail to prevent the widespread and devastating systems breakdown which had just occurred? And why was an unfamiliar circuit-board with two small cylindrical objects clipped to it still wedged under the smoking remains of the main power distribution console?

In his tiny cabin behind the Palm Court entertainment lounge and oblivious to all of this frenetic activity, the Magician shifted slightly on his bunk and stared at the ceiling. Being an entertainer on the luxury flagship of an interstellar fleet sounded so exciting, so romantic, so.... well you know! In fact, it was tedious in the extreme. The tedium was a direct consequence of his lack of status. As an entertainer he was accorded none of the privileges enjoyed by the passengers. Many of the ship's facilities were denied to crew and other cruise line employees. But he was no less unwelcome in those parts of the ship that were off limits to the paying customers. The ship's officers considered that anyone who was not entitled to wear Merchant Space Navy insignia must be a lower form of life, and they made it clear that any intrusion into areas like the officers' mess or the crew recreation areas would be treated as provocative behaviour.

The Magician wanted to book a table at the Star Lounge Restaurant. The galling thing was that he wasn't allowed to. It wasn't that he was hungry. Getting fed was no problem. He had only to press a transceiver stud and talk to the galley. Within minutes a perfectly acceptable meal would be delivered to his cabin. The problem was, the Magician didn't want to eat alone. What he really wanted to do was ask Gloria, his stage assistant, out for a romantic candle lit dinner.

He and Gloria had been working the cruise liners for several years. They were a great team. She was beautiful, intelligent and sympathetic. She knew his act inside out. Privately, he was convinced that she could probably do every single trick - maybe better than he could. But she never ever overstepped the boundaries of her own role. Instead she worked hard to make him look better than he really was. He'd have given up this life years ago, but he didn't want to give up Gloria. He snuggled back against his pillow and thought about Gloria's wonderful smile.

"Gloria," he told the ceiling, "I love you!" Trouble was, telling the ceiling was as far as he ever got. If only he could take her to the ship's most expensive restaurant. Spoil her with exotic alien dishes. Pamper her with scented wines from far off worlds. Perhaps then, in the afterglow of post-epicurean contentment, he could pluck up the courage to propose to her. To suggest that they give up this interminable living out of suitcases and settle down on their home world to live normal, ordinary, wonderfully boring lives of domestic bliss. But he wasn't allowed in the blasted restaurant. You can't fete the woman of your dreams in a utility cabin that's two metres square.

This was getting him nowhere. The Magician decided to amble over to the rehearsal rooms and practise pulling a struggling member of the genus Lagomorpha[1] out of an apparently empty crewman's helmet.

---

[1]A brown-furred rodent common on certain agricultural planets and identifiable by its long ears and powder-puff tail.

Chapter 2

The cat was tired of lying on her bunk. (Since she was a cat, that should give you some idea of how long she'd been lying there.) She decided to go and explore. Surely there would be something interesting happening somewhere on the largest star cruiser in the Yellow Star fleet. She slipped through the door and found herself standing in a corridor. It was exactly like the corridor that seems to run down the backbone of every twentieth century hospital. For a start off, it was long - very long. It was so long that before perspective could bring all its parallels to a point, it just faded into the misty distance. Its walls were broken at intervals by doors, big impressive double doors of the kind that swing shut behind you of their own accord, and they all looked just the same. Set into the resilient shiny grey floor covering was a shower of coloured arrows, all pointing the same way. Wherever you were going on the Space Cruiser Gigantean, this was how you got there. All you had to do was follow the arrows whose colour corresponded to your destination and Bob was your uncle. The drawback, of course, was that no-one (especially the crew) had ever managed to decrypt the colour code. As a consequence, the exact nature of Bob's familial inter-relationships was, and always would be, an impenetrable secret. The largest arrows were red so the cat decided to follow those.

She walked for what seemed like several minutes. Nothing appeared to have changed. The corridor still stretched off into infinity, the doors still looked identical. The cat began to suffer from a feeling that she hadn't in fact moved at all.

As she passed a pair of doors on her right they were pushed open. A handcart emerged, pushed by a sturdy crewman wearing regulation fatigues. He was soaked in sweat. From the hot, dark, moist depths behind the door came an overpowering smell of rot and decay. Obviously she had found the fungus farm, where the raw material for most of the ship's food originated. The cat decided not to go in - it wasn't that long until dinner.

Another pair of doors opened to her left. A small and very harassed looking maintenance robot scurried around her and headed off up the corridor, murmuring agitatedly to itself. As the doors began to swing closed, she slipped inside and sat down whilst taking a look around. Huge banks of machinery rose on each side. The deck in here was metallic, the air was full of ozone and the light was red and somehow menacing. At a workbench a few paces away, the chief engineer, a four armed cyclopean from a star on the other side of the Horse Head Nebula was giving a thorough chewing out to Temporary Acting Ensign (Third Class) Weasel Crinkler.

"Ye stupid wee spalpeen! Have ye no got the brains ye were born wi? Did ye no consider even for a moment the drrreadful consequences of what ye were doing?"

"I'm sorry Chief! It was my grade school science project. We were supposed to build a battery charger and charge up two penlight batteries with it by tomorrow's lesson."

"Aye, of course ye were," breathed the enraged officer. "And I'm quite sure the teacher told ye to connect it up to the primary engine powerr bus, now didn't she?"

"I'm sorry Chief, I was just trying to save the effort of turning that little dynamo thingy that she gave us. I thought that..."

"No ye didnae," bellowed the Engineer. "If ye'd thought at all ye'd have realised that two tichy ni-cads cannae absorb the total electrical output of a starship's engines withoot even a resistorr in the line! It'll take four or five hours to re-align the warp drive, and the mass proximity detectors are burned to a crisp! There could be anything at all oot there and we'd know nothing at all aboot it!" [1]

The cat slipped quietly out of the Engineering Section leaving Weasel alone with his Nemesis.

A little further down the corridor, the cat reached an intersection. Arrows now split off the main path and ran left or right as well as the ones that continued to point straight on. The large red arrows, of course, pointed straight on. And left. And right. "Well," thought the

[1]There is indeed something out there, and we now have a clue to a momentous happening which is still some way in the ship's future.

cat, “at least it looks as though I’m going somewhere that isn’t easy to miss.”

At the end of the right hand corridor was another pair of doors. Stencilled across them in gold paint were the words, ‘SEVEN STARBOARD’. "Oh well,” thought the cat, “in for a credit, in for an imperial.” She slipped through the doors and found herself in a large and comfortably furnished lounge. Small groups of passengers were sitting around tables, sipping drinks and nibbling a variety of confections. On the stage, a red-nosed comic was re-living his most common nightmare, the audience with no sense of humour. The comic’s name was Betel and he was sweating profusely.

“I had a long and distinguished career in the Helvetian Space Navy you know. Oh yes, I fought with Admiral Massokitz at Rigel 5, I fought with Admiral Di Saad at Aldebaran and I fought with Admiral Mutillato at the Crab Nebula Uprising. (Dramatic pause). I never could get on with Admirals!”

There was an embarrassed giggle from the back, which might or might not have been a response to the carefully delivered gag. Of course, Betel knew what was wrong. The audience wasn’t intellectual enough for his brand of humour. Perhaps he should drop his trousers. That usually got a laugh. From the female members of the audience at least, he thought bitterly.

“Thank you Madam", he said to the giggler. “Shouldn’t there be another of you nearer the front? I’m sure I paid for two!” That raised a few smiles. “Of course", said Betel following up quickly, “You’re all very lucky to have me aboard! Oh yes! I am the man who saved the lives of the entire crew and all the passengers of a cruise liner just like this one only two standard months ago. How? I’m very glad you asked me that! I’ll tell you how. I shot the cook!” There was a scattering of laughter, redoubled when a stout gentleman at a table near the front belched loudly. Betel’s nightmare receded. The audience were warming to him after all.

Sitting at a table a few feet from the stage was a strikingly attractive woman with blonde hair and a figure that might have been described as statuesque[1]. She was probably in her mid to late thirties but with bone structure like hers she'd look wonderful until way into old age. She was staring at her untouched drink with an intensity that suggested that she wasn't seeing it. She also wasn't hearing the comic's rather threadbare patter.

She was thinking that the time had come for direct action. Five years ago she had identified the man she was going to marry. Ever since then she had been waiting for him to pop the question. Well, she'd waited long enough! Multiple plans of attack, created during endless lonely nights in a succession of tiny cabins, swirled through her memory.

Plan A was the old fallback. Respond to the lewd advances of the ship's most obvious Lothario and wait for her intended's jealousy to do the rest. Of course it wouldn't work. Her intended was such a caring, sympathetic man that he would hide his bitter disappointment behind a synthetic smile and sincerely wish her every happiness before going off to cry out his frustration in his lonely bunk.

Plan B played itself out in her imagination. The drunken old fool that she had hired to play the part of her outraged and gun-toting father was pretty convincing. Unfortunately he had forgotten his lines and was improvising. When her intended protested that there had been no impropriety, instead of marching him into the chapel at gunpoint, the old fool declared that he believed him and even insisted on buying him a drink before stumbling off into the darkness, never to be seen again. "No," she thought, "I mustn't leave it up to someone else. I've got to do this myself!"

Plan C entailed her entering his room at 1.00am dressed only in the most diaphanous of her hitherto unseen collection of sexy nighties. Roused from sleep, his delighted smile as his eyes took in her almost unconcealed charms would instantly turn to a look of guilty alarm. "My dear," he would say (dear sweet innocent man that he was), "you shouldn't be here dressed like that. We're not married!" At that moment she would jerk the rope concealed in her left hand whereupon

---

[1]Mind you, any red-blooded male would probably find more appropriate language like,"Ohgoodgriefwouldyagetaloadofthat!" or "Zwing!" He would probably also drool, click his heels in the air and howl at the moon rather a lot.

the gagged and handcuffed captain of the ship would stumble through the door, to conduct an on the spot wedding ceremony (only just in time).

That one wouldn't work either. It's almost impossible to kidnap the captain of a starship, especially when dressed in a diaphanous nightie[1], and even if she managed it she'd probably spend her honeymoon and the rest of her married life in solitary confinement in a penal colony somewhere on the edge of the galaxy.

It rather looked as if plan D was going to have to suffice. The Gigantean's next time-tabled port of call was at the planet Termagant in three days time. Customs there were a little different from the Galactic norm. It was a culture dominated by aggressive feminism. It was also a planet where women were always safe on the streets. The only men allowed out unaccompanied were the eunuchs. Any man in possession of his, er, faculties had to be accompanied by his wife. If an unmarried couple were challenged, the only acceptable excuse (and incidentally, way of preserving those faculties) was that the couple were on their way to the registry office to get married. It wouldn't be easy to persuade him to go gawking at the sights planetside but she thought it might just work!

At the thought of finally persuading her man to marry her, Gloria's face lit up in the smile which the Magician so often dreamed about. Gloria's smile could stimulate glands that doctors still hadn't discovered. When aimed in the approximate direction of any red-blooded male it relegated the libido enhancing effect of love potion number 9 to the same level as a cold shower.

A waiter with a large tray of drinks balanced above his head caught the full unfocussed blast of Gloria's happiness. He wouldn't mind the dressing down that he was certainly going to get from the Head Waiter. He wouldn't care about the huge sum that would be docked from his meagre wage for spillages and breakages. He would happily work the extra hours demanded in punishment for his carelessness. None of these things would spoil his euphoria - Gloria had smiled at him!

---

[1]The kidnapper, of course! What any captain wears in the privacy of his sleeping quarters is no-one's business but his own.

Chapter 3

The Captain of the Gigantean touched a transmission stud in the arm of his chair and cleared his throat. "Bridge to Engineering," he said.

"Aye sorr, Chief Engineer here."

"Mr Gael, how is the work on the mass proximity detectors coming along? This is a relatively crowded sector and I don't much relish the thought of being out here with no warning of what's sharing our space."

"I should have them back on line in another twenty minutes or so sorr. That burrst of raw power that went down their line de-coupled every transducer in the array, and I've had tae send someone oot there to replace them manually."

The Captain gasped. "Good grief man! How the blazes did you find a volunteer willing to go out onto the hull with our particle shields still down?"

It wasnae hard at all sorr. Mr Crinkler seemed particularly eager to get out of Engineering for a while, if ye take ma meaning?"

On the big forward view screen something dark occluded a few hundred stars.

The Captain glanced at the screen. Working from a later reconstruction of the automatic log it's fairly certain that he said, "What the b............. "

An enormous cometary mass composed mainly of dirty ice[1] smashed into the bows of the Gigantean at 17.13 hours ship's time. It instantly pulverized the bridge, the crew quarters, the galley and the nursery (thankfully un-used on this trip). It also ripped apart the library, the observation dome, the communications room, the turkish baths, and the zero gee swimming pool. It answered the prayers of the fundamentalist Assembly of Galactic Theosophists when it annihilated

---

[1] A sort of interplanetary iceberg.

the virtual reality adult entertainment booths. Seconds later it also atomized their small and expensively austere chapel.

As is usual in disasters of this kind, every piece of electrical equipment in Engineering immediately exploded in a coruscating firework display of sparks, and girders began to fall from the roof.

In the quarter gee ballroom (if you've never danced the jitterbug in quarter gee you haven't lived) the robot orchestra was playing the latest hit number from the colony on Rigel 5, "Come and share my habitat module, oh yeah!"

Within seconds, airtight doors had slammed into place at strategic positions along the length of the hull. In each section red signs began to flash out their hypnotic message, ABANDON SHIP <blink> ABANDON SHIP <blink> ABANDON SHIP <blink> ABANDON SHIP <blink> - you get the picture.

As the dust began to settle, a tannoy system wheezed into life and a computerised voice announced, "GOOD AFTERNOON LADIES AND GENTLEMEN. THE CAPTAIN PRESENTS HIS COMPLIMENTS AND REQUESTS THAT YOU MAKE YOUR WAY AS QUICKLY AS POSSIBLE TO THE NEAREST ESCAPE CRAFT STATION. THERE IS NO CAUSE FOR PANIC. PLEASE MAKE YOUR WAY TO THE NEAREST ESCAPE CRAFT STATION. THANK YOU."

The Magician painfully heaved aside the remains of the doors to Seven Starboard. The Entertainment Lounge was in darkness. He selected the flashlight accessory on his Helvetian Space Navy penknife and shone it around the room, looking for Gloria. "Where the hell is the nearest escape craft station?" he demanded.

"SILLY ME." said the tannoy. "THE NEAREST ESCAPE CRAFT STATION MAY BE LOCATED BY FOLLOWING THE BIG RED ARROWS ON THE FLOOR. HAVE A NICE DAY."

The Magician lifted a heavy table with bleeding hands. The feet that had been sticking out from underneath were not Gloria's and they weren't going to do any more walking.

A white face with a prominent red nose and a permanently mournful expression appeared from beneath a pile of debris. It was followed by a scrawny body wearing a rumpled suit. "Give me a hand," Betel said, "there's a woman under here".

Gloria wasn't badly hurt, just a little bruised and battered. "Why are we supposed to be abandoning ship," she muttered. "I thought this liner was supposed to be, you know, un-whatsit-able!"

"I don't follow you," said the Magician. "What do you mean un-whatsit-able?"

"It's the biggest they've ever built," Gloria explained. "It's fitted with every safety device known to science. All its systems are multi-redundant, whatever that means. It has air tight doors at each corridor intersection. It can't be damaged so badly that it won't support life. It's so safe, they didn't even bother with a full complement of life boats."

"Somehow," said Betel, "I just knew you were going to say something like that! How many lifeboats does it have, exactly?"

"Two."

"TWO?" screamed Betel. "TWO? There are over two thousand people on this behemoth and they've provided TWO lifeboats?"

"Please," said the Magician gently. "Please tell me that they take over a thousand people each!"

"I don't know," said Gloria thoughtfully. "Computer?"

"HELLO THERE," said the tannoy. "CAN I ASSIST YOU IN ANY WAY?"

"How many persons will each of the ship's lifeboats hold?"

"QUERY NOT UNDERSTOOD," said the tannoy. "WHAT ARE LIFEBOATS?"

"Oh good grief," said Gloria. "Escape craft, little space ships with atmospheric capability, so that we can land on a nice friendly planet. You know the sort of thing?"

"OH, THOSE! THEY CAN CARRY A MAXIMUM OF TEN PERSONS".

"TEN?" screamed Betel. "Ten EACH?"

"YES SIR, BUT THEY ARE REALLY MUCH MORE COMFORTABLE IF ONLY SIX PERSONS ARE CARRIED, SINCE THE LIFE SUPPORT SYSTEMS ARE REALLY QUITE MINIMAL."

“Come on,” said the Magician in a tone of voice that suggested the exertion of iron control. “I think we’d better try to get to the lifeboats before they’re full!”

Chapter 4

The second lieutenant guarding escape craft number one was polite but insistent. The standing instructions which he had been given said that he was to allow only women and children to board the craft, and he was going to obey his instructions even if they killed him.[1]

"Look!" said Betel, grinding his teeth as he attempted to communicate with a thinking person who, after countless years of naval training, probably no longer existed. "There are no children on board this ship - right?"

"That is correct sir."

"And only one person in every hundred aboard this liner is female - right?"

"That is also correct sir."

"You have just admitted that we are the only people to have arrived at this escape station - right?"

"That is correct sir."

"And the escape craft will automatically launch in two minutes - right?"

"That is also correct sir."

"Then for crying out loud - don't you think that perhaps we'd better all get on board before it leaves?"

"I am very sorry sir," the officer's weapon didn't exactly point at Betel but it looked as if it wanted to. "My orders are that only women and children shall be allowed to board this vehicle."

"Please Gloria," said the Magician as he struggled to restrain the by now homicidal Betel. "Please get on the lifeboat."

"I can't just go and leave you behind," sobbed Gloria.

---

[1]Which, in point of fact, they were bound to do.

The Magician took the white time-locked flower from his buttonhole and pressed it into Gloria's hand. "Please go," he said. "If you don't save yourself, I won't be able to live with myself."

Betel tried to wriggle far enough out of the Magician's grip to bite the officer. "Not a problem that's likely to trouble you for very long," he snarled.

"Please madam," said the apparently impassive crewman. "Please get on board before it's too late." He hustled Gloria into the airlock and spun the wheel.

A klaxon sounded. There was a loud detonation and the deck jumped. The tannoy wheezed into life. "ALL ESCAPE CRAFT HAVE BEEN LAUNCHED," it said. "HULL INTEGRITY IS COMPROMISED. ESTIMATED TIME UNTIL CATASTROPHIC STRUCTURAL FAILURE IS THREE MINUTES AND TWENTY-SIX SECONDS. HAVE A NICE DAY." The second lieutenant raised the laser pistol to his forehead. "God, I hate my job," he said and pulled the trigger.

Betel stopped struggling. The Magician released his grip and the comic slumped to the deck. "Computer," said the Magician. "Is there any other way to leave this liner?"

"FOLLOW THE LARGE RED ARROWS TO ESCAPE LOCKER 13," said the tannoy. "CLIMB INTO THE PLASTIC ENVELOPES YOU WILL FIND INSIDE THE LOCKER. WHEN THEY ARE SEALED YOU MUST PULL THE GREEN LEVER."

Less than two minutes later, the two entertainers were floating in space. Each of them was enclosed in a globe of tough transparent plastic with aerosol manoeuvring jets and manipulatory appendages like armoured rubber gloves set into the surface at various points. The view was completely unimpeded by the plastic envelope and as a result the feeling of being naked and unprotected in space was added to the already dreadful sensation of vertigo.

The Magician had been listening to the screaming for some while before he realised that he was its source. He bit off the sound and breathed deeply.

He forced himself to open his eyes and look around. With a shudder he scanned quickly across the spreading cloud of debris which was all that remained of the fifty thousand tonne flagship of the Yellow Star fleet. Some twenty metres to his left was another escape envelope like his own. Floating in its approximate centre was the tightly curled foetal shape of Betel, the red-nosed comic.

Betel obviously needed someone to talk to but the Magician had a feeling that this primitive device wouldn't be equipped with a radio. A quick check around the plastic bubble confirmed his assumption. Oh well then, time to amble over there. A quick squirt from one of the aerosols started his little craft travelling in approximately the right direction. It was only moving very slowly, but he had a feeling that slowly was about all he could handle at the moment.

The next question was, what should he do when his ball reached Betel's? He didn't think that he was going to be skilful enough to stop in exactly the right place. Actually, he realised, stopping wasn't dreadfully important. All he had to do was dock with the other ball. Dock. How does one plastic beach ball *dock* with another one? He slipped his hands into two of the rubber glove thingies that stuck out from his envelope in all directions. Slowly, s l o w l y , the two balloons came together. He made a grab for one of the gloves that studded the outside of Betel's envelope like the udders on a dairy farmer's worst nightmare. He held on tight.

The two giant beach balls did just what two beach balls meeting in mid-flight are supposed to do. They bounced. It was in the Magician's mind that they were weightless in space and, of course, he was right. What he hadn't given enough consideration to, was that weightless and mass-less are not the same thing. As the two vibrating envelopes attempted to wobble off in opposite directions, the strain of holding them and their human cargos together was almost more than his poor tortured fingers could bear.

As the oscillations died away he pulled until the walls of the two plastic globes were touching, pressing together tightly. "BETEL", he yelled.

"Aaaargh! Eh? Wassat?" Betel was still curled up tighter than a hedgehog in a badger's dining room.

"Come on Betel, it's me - the Magician. Open your eyes".

"OPEN MY EYES?" Betel was close to hysteria. "Have you gone stark raving MAD? Have you seen what's out there?"

"There's nothing out there to be frightened of," said the Magician, gently.

"For crying out loud," Betel gibbered. Don't you understand? It's precisely all that nothing out there that's frightening me!"

"Look, old chap, it's just like standing on a high cliff. It's all right so long as you don't look down."

"Don't look down? Don't look DOWN? For Pete's sake! Which way is down?"

The Magician's fingers were numb. "Down is past your feet," he said patiently.

Betel half opened his eyes, screamed and clamped them shut again. "If down is past my feet," he groaned, "then what the hell is past yours?"

Belatedly, the Magician realised that he and Betel were not the same way up. "Betel," he said, "I don't think I can hold on to your balloon much longer. I've lost all the feeling in my fingers. If you don't help me, then our balloons are going to drift apart and you'll be on your own. Make up your own mind, but don't take too long."

Betel gritted his teeth. He opened one eye. It rolled around a bit. He opened the other. He whimpered. "Wh, wha what do you want me to do?" he asked.

"Put your hand into one of those gloves and try to grab my balloon."

Betel managed to get a grip on one of the Magician's gloves at only the second attempt. "What's that over there?" he asked.

"Over where?" said his saviour, looking in the indicated direction. "It's a lifeboat - that's what it is! Betel, you're my friend for life!" As Betel strained to hold the two plastic balls together, the Magician released squirts of aerosol gas, first to stop them spinning, and then to begin the slow journey across to the lifeboat. "Don't go away Gloria," he shouted, "- we're coming!"

"Hey! You're good at this!" Betel was impressed by the way his friend manoeuvred the balloons over to the lifeboat and would have applauded when they slowed to a stop just before contact with the airlock,[1] except that both his hands were busy keeping the two fragile envelopes together. The Magician reached out with a gloved hand and pushed a button on the panel beside the airlock. It slid open. Holding onto a handrail with one hand he shoved Betel's beach ball into the lock.

The airlock was designed to accommodate five people at once. One escape balloon filled it to capacity. As the lock cycled, the Magician hung on to the rail outside and rehearsed what he was going to say when Gloria rushed into his arms. Something casual perhaps? "Hello my dear, we've got to stop meeting like this." Not bad!

At last the status light glowed green. He opened the airlock door and swung his balloon through the opening. There was one terrifying moment when the plastic snagged on the frame and he was convinced that it would tear, but the skin was obviously far tougher than it looked. Before the air pressure in the lock reached one atmosphere he unzipped the balloon and he threw himself through the inner door before it had completely opened.

His plan for the dramatic reunion with Gloria foundered at two points. The first was that she was supposed to rush into his arms. Actually, it was he who burst out of the airlock crying, "Gloria! I was afraid I'd never see you ag ...." The second problem was that the lifeboat's sole female occupant was at that moment sitting comfortably on the pilot's chair, licking one of her front paws.

---

[1]The Magician had learned his lesson. If he never bounced a ball again, it would still be at least a hundred years too soon!

Chapter 5

"Computer," said the Magician. "Where is Gloria?"

The rusty voice of the computer crackled from the wall. "HELLO." it said, "I'M GLAD YOU MADE IT SIRS. YOUR FRIEND IS ABOARD ESCAPE CRAFT NUMBER ONE."

"Then," reasoned the Magician, "this must be escape craft number two?"

"YES SIR, ESCAPE CRAFT NUMBER ONE IS JUST BEGINNING THE COURSE ADJUSTMENTS NEEDED IN ORDER TO RENDEZVOUS WITH THE ONLY TYPE M WORLD IN THIS SYSTEM. AS SOON AS I HAVE MADE ALL THE NECESSARY CALCULATIONS, WE WILL BE FOLLOWING."

"Computer." Betel's interruption sounded like someone nervously clearing his throat. "This planet, what's it like?"

"WELL SIR," the computer paused as if searching for words that even a layman could understand, "IT IS IN ORBIT AROUND A RATHER ORDINARY YELLOW DWARF STAR. IT HAS AN EQUATORIAL RADIUS APPROACHING SIX AND A HALF MILLION METRES AND MASSES ALMOST 6 TIMES 10^{24} KILOGRAMMES. IT IS COMPOSED MOSTLY OF SILICA WITH ALL THE USUAL IMPURITIES OVER A CORE OF MOLTEN NICKLE IRON. ITS SURFACE IS MOSTLY COVERED IN LIQUID WATER. IT HAS A BREATHEABLE ATMOSPHERE WHICH IS LARGELY NITROGEN WITH ABOUT FIFTEEN PERCENT OXYGEN, ALSO SOME CARBON DIOXIDE AND WATER VAPOUR. THERE ARE TRACES OF OTHER GASES, BUT NOTHING HARMFUL. IT SPINS ON ITS AXIS IN AROUND ONE STANDARD DAY AND ITS TEMPERATURE VARIES FROM 185^0 ABSOLUTE AT ONE OF ITS POLES TO SOME 323^0 ABSOLUTE AT THE EQUATOR."

"Yes, thank you very much," snapped Betel, "but what's it like?"

"It sounds very much like my home world," the Magician mused. "It has life, I suppose?"

"OH YES, SIR. THE SEAS ARE TEEMING WITH LIFE, THE LAND IS COVERED WITH VEGETATION AND THERE IS A WIDE RANGE OF LAND DWELLING FAUNA, RANGING IN SIZE FROM MICROSCOPIC STRINGS OF DNA UP TO LUMBERING GIANTS WEIGHING SEVERAL TONNES. CREATURES

BELONGING TO AT LEAST THREE DIFFERENT EVOLUTIONARY STRAINS HAVE LEARNED TO FLY, AND EVERY ECOLOGICAL NICHE HAS A CREATURE TO TAKE ADVANTAGE OF IT."

"Very, very much like my home world," repeated the Magician. "I don't suppose it has intelligent life?"

The computer hesitated for a moment. "NORMALLY, SIR, INFORMATION ABOUT PRIMITIVE INTELLIGENT LIFE FORMS IS CLASSIFIED. HOWEVER, SINCE WE ARE FORCED TO LAND ON THE PLANET, YOU WILL SOON KNOW MORE THAN IS CONTAINED IN MY MEMORY BANKS AND I CAN SEE NO REASON TO WITHHOLD THE INFORMATION YOU SEEK. "

All three passengers leaned forward to hear the answer.

"THE DOMINANT LIFE FORM ON THE PLANET IS A MAMMALIAN BIPED. ACCORDING TO THE GALACTIC FEDERATION'S DEFINITION IT IS HUMANOID TO 98%. THE BASIC UNIT OF THEIR SOCIETY IS THE EXTENDED FAMILY, AND THEIR CULTURE IS PREDOMINENTLY TRIBAL, ALTHOUGH CIVILIZATION IS DEVELOPING IN SOME AREAS OF THEIR WORLD. THEIR TECHNOLOGY IS PRIMITIVE. THEY HAVE BEGUN TO WORK METALS, GOLD, SILVER, COPPER AND TIN. THEY HAVE LEARNED TO MAKE BRONZE AND USE IT TO MAKE TOOLS AND WEAPONS. THEY TRADE WIDELY ACROSS THEIR WORLD AND HAVE EXPLORED ALL BUT ONE OF THEIR TEMPERATE CONTINENTS. THE PLANET IS CLASSIFIED AS OFF LIMITS EXCEPT IN EMERGENCIES AND NO CULTURAL OR TECHNOLOGICAL POLLUTION MUST BE PERMITTED. IT IS EXPECTED THAT THESE PEOPLE WILL DEVELOP ACCORDING TO THE NORM FOR THEIR TYPE AND WILL ACHIEVE SPACE TRAVEL CAPABILITY IN SOME THREE TO FOUR THOUSAND OF THEIR YEARS. THIS ASSUMES THAT THEY DO NOT DESTROY THEMSELVES FIRST IN THE PROCESS OF MASTERING NUCLEAR OR BIOLOGICAL TECHNOLOGIES."

"It occurs to me," said the Magician, "that there's likely to be rather a lot of technological pollution when they find a fully equipped escape vehicle lying around, complete with a chatty computer that seems to know just about everything that they're supposed to learn for themselves over the next four thousand years!"

"THAT SIR," said the rusty voice of the computer, "IS WHY YOU HAVE ONLY TEN MINUTES TO VACATE THIS VEHICLE AFTER WE MAKE OUR LANDING. WHEN THAT PERIOD OF TIME HAS ELAPSED I SHALL

AUTOMATICALLY SELF DESTRUCT. I WOULD RECOMMEND THAT YOU TRY TO BE AT LEAST TWO HUNDRED METRES AWAY WHEN MY APOTHEOSIS OCCURS."

Betel groaned and cradled his head in his hands. "So," he queried, "you seem to be saying that we're going to be trapped on this backward planet full of primitive savages for the rest of our lives with no modern amenities and no hope of rescue because it's off limits. Does that just about sum it up?"

"IT'S NOT QUITE THAT BAD SIR. THE PEOPLE ARE REALLY QUITE FRIENDLY, AND YOUR UNIVERSAL TRANSLATOR IMPLANT WILL COPE ADMIRABLY WITH THEIR LANGUAGE. AS FOR RESCUE - YELLOW STAR LINE NEVER ABANDONS A PASSENGER. IN THE LAST FEW SECONDS OF MY EXISTENCE, AS MY ENGINES REACH PEAK OVERLOAD, ALL OF THEIR CONSIDERABLE OUTPUT WILL BE FOCUSSED INTO ONE COHERENT LIGHT PULSE WHICH I WILL DIRECT TOWARDS THE NEAREST REGIONAL BOOKING OFFICE. RESCUE WILL BE HERE BEFORE YOU HAVE A CHANCE TO MISS ME."

"It'll be a long time before I get around to missing you," muttered Betel ominously.

The cat stretched and directed her amber gaze toward the console. "Computer," she growled, "are there cats on this world?"

"Doesn't seem likely does it?" said Betel.

"Why not?" asked the cat. "We are superbly suited to survive in a wide range of environments, and are so adaptable that we are the logical outcome and pinnacle of evolution on almost any M type world."

"There aren't any cats on my world," said Betel.

Then I pity your world," said the cat. "Computer, what is the answer to my question?"

"THERE ARE CATS ON THIS WORLD," said the computer, "BUT WITH A FEW EXCEPTIONS THEY ARE SAVAGE AND ALTHOUGH RELATIVELY INTELLIGENT, THEY ARE NOT BELIEVED TO BE SAPIENT."

An orange lamp on the console began to flash urgently.

"WHILE WE HAVE BEEN TALKING, I HAVE COMPLETED THE

CALCULATION OF OUR COURSE ADJUSTMENT. MAY I SUGGEST THAT YOU ALL GET ONTO THE ACCELERATION COUCHES NOW? THERE MAY BE SOME DISCOMFORT AS THIS SMALL CRAFT IS NOT EQUIPPED WITH AN INERTIAL DAMPING FIELD."

Moments later the engines fired and the escape vehicle began to accelerate towards one of the points of light visible on the viewscreen.

Chapter 6

As Gloria trudged away from the smoking wreckage of her escape craft, she couldn't help thinking of the Magician and the way he had insisted that she save herself, even as he faced certain death. "Oh God," she said to her now certainly deceased sweetheart, "I loved you!"

"It's the first sign you know," said a voice behind her.

Gloria spun around. "What the hell …," she began.

Standing behind her was a slightly overweight middle-aged woman. She was dressed in a brown homespun woollen dress with a shawl over her shoulders. Her greying hair was caught up in a sprang[1] hairnet and hanging at her waist was a small leather bag.

"What's the first sign? The first sign of what?" Gloria was off balance.

"Talking to yourself." The other woman had a pleasant voice. "It's the first sign that you're going off your rocker!"

Despite herself, Gloria laughed. "Hello," she said, "my name's Gloria."

"Hello yourself," said her self-appointed psychoanalyst, "everybody calls me Old Meg."

There was a short pause as the two women sized each other up. "Here," said Meg, pointing to the column of smoke, "was that your chariot?"

"Yes," said Gloria, deciding that honesty was likely to be the best policy, "it was."

"Oh, right," replied Meg, "then it'll be some sort of magic, I suppose?"

"Magic?" Gloria was puzzled.

---

[1]A kind of net, knotted on a springy frame which holds it under tension, so that when finished the fabric retains some elasticity.

“The flying chariot,” Meg wasn’t going to give up. “It must be some kind of magic.”

“No,” said Gloria, “it’s just technology - the application of science.”

“That’s what I said,” Meg replied. ”Magic!”

Gloria began to wonder what the universal translator implant was actually saying on her behalf. “But,” she said, “I don’t believe in magic.”

No-one who had spent the hours that she had spent stuffing bunches of collapsible flowers, decks of cards and assorted members of the genus Lagomorpha into a conjuror’s stage suit, could still reasonably be expected to believe in magic.

Meg laughed. She closed her eyes and murmured a few half audible words. In her outstretched hands a small brown bird appeared. She opened her hands and tossed the bird into the air. It flew away.

Gloria smiled appreciatively. It was very smoothly done, she had to admit. A variation of the vanishing coin trick would seem to be appropriate, she thought. She reached down and plucked a small yellow flower from the grass at her feet.

“What’s this called?” she asked.

“That’s a goldeneye,” said Meg.

Gloria closed her hands over the flower and then opened them again. The flower was gone.

Meg smiled. “A child’s magic,” she murmured.

Gloria tried hard to look outraged. “Why have you stolen my flower?” she demanded.

Meg looked surprised. “Stolen?” she said.

“Why yes!” Gloria seized the pouch from Meg’s belt and tipped it up. A lock of hair, a bone needle, two nicely coloured pebbles, one with a hole in it, an animal’s tooth and two identical goldeneyes fell into the palm of her hand.

Meg sat down on the grass and laughed heartily. “A merry jape,” she chortled. Surely you are one of us - sister.”

Two things were puzzling Gloria. Firstly, why was Meg suddenly calling her sister? Secondly, why were there two goldeneyes in her hand when she had palmed only one?

Chapter 7

Betel woke slowly. The light that was trying to crowbar its way past his eyelids was blue and he could feel a gentle breeze on his skin. "If I'm dead," he thought, "this doesn't feel much like Hell." He experimentally opened one eye. Hovering in front of him was a vision from one of his better dreams. A face with big hazel eyes, long lashes, red bee-stung lips and a cascade of shining chestnut hair. "If this is Hell," he told her, "it's been given a very bad press!" "Hello," said the vision, in a voice that reminded him of honey and elderflowers. "My name is Bryony. How does your poor nose feel?"

"I'm glad you decided to join us," said the voice of the Magician from somewhere off to his right. "You've been unconscious for rather a long time."

Betel painfully levered himself up onto one elbow and looked around. He was lying in a field of gently waving grass. Off to his right beyond his smiling friend was a patch of woodland, whilst the ground on his left sloped away from him. He suspected that there would be water at the bottom. About half a kilometre away in the direction indicated by his outstretched legs was a column of greasy looking smoke. He pointed towards it.

"Was that the escape craft?"

The Magician glanced at Bryony. "Yes," he admitted, "the light show was very impressive."

"How did I get here?"

The voice of the cat came from somewhere behind him. "Your friend carried you," she said, "over his shoulder, like a sack of vegetables."

"Give me a hand," said Betel, "I've got to get up."

"Oh no!" Bryony's restraining hand on his chest made his heart skip several beats. "Daddy's gone back to the village to get a litter and some friends to carry it. You've had a nasty fall and I'm going to take care of you."

Betel laid back and thought how very fortunate he was.

Bryony held his hand until the litter arrived. In Betel's opinion it came much too quickly. Two muscular young men wearing rough woollen tunics lifted him, surprisingly gently, onto what turned out to be a woven split willow hurdle with a layer of straw spread over it. They and two others took a corner each and everyone set out for the village.

The older man supporting the corner next to Betel's right shoulder turned out to be Bryony's father. He told Betel that his name was Chive and that he was a cooper.

"Excuse me?" said Betel, who had no idea what a cooper was.

"A cooper," Chive repeated, and then seeing the puzzled expression on Betel's face, "a barrel maker - you know?"

Betel didn't know, but it occurred to him that ignorance of everyday common knowledge was a certain way to make the natives suspicious. "Of course," he said. "Silly of me. It must have been that bump on the head!"

Chive made sympathetic clicking noises with his tongue. "A bit of rest, and a good rub with my Bryony's home-made liniment," he said, "and you'll be as good as new. We're nearly there now, here's the village."

The village was surrounded by a ditch and a fence made of hurdles like the one that Betel was currently occupying. Inside the oval enclosure were about a dozen large round houses. Each had a low outer wall of wattle and daub and a tall conical roof of rough thatch. Several smaller buildings turned out to be stores, workshops and animal shelters.

"You must be my guests," said Chive. "Bryony and I have had the house to ourselves since my wife died, and there's plenty of room."

There was indeed plenty of room. The house was based on two concentric circles of upright posts, set firmly into the ground. Cross pieces linked the uprights of each circle. Rafters rested on the outside circle, climbed up over the taller inner circle and met at the apex of the roof. Wicker hurdles formed an outer wall and divided the space between the two circles of posts into cells or cubicles. Some of these were used for sleeping, some for storage. In the centre of the house a fire burned all the time. It not only provided warmth in cold weather and a hearth for cooking, but it also lit the interior. A house like this could be home to an extended family of a dozen people spanning three or even four generations.

Chive settled the Magician and Betel into two compartments close to his own on the side of the house nearest to the door. The cat stalked off to curl up on the hearth in front of the fire. Bryony appeared a little later with a small jug containing an infusion of herbs in an oily base. She rubbed it into all of the places where Betel was bruised and to his great surprise it really seemed to help.

Later, when Bryony was sitting by the fire basting,[1] the two travellers were left alone for the first time since their arrival on the planet.

"I don't understand," said Betel, "why hasn't anyone asked us where we're from, or how we got here?"

"I think it's something to do with this planet," replied the Magician. "When I carried you away from the escape craft, I bumped into Chive and Bryony. A minute later, the craft self-destructed. Chive looked at me and asked me if it had been our chariot? I was so surprised that I said yes, and do you know what he said then?"

"No," said Betel, "what did he say?"

"Oh right you are," said the Magician in a fair imitation of Chive's voice, "then it'll be some sort of magic I suppose."

"Weird," Betel agreed. "There's another thing that's puzzling me. If there are no sapient cats on this planet, why does no-one look surprised when the cat speaks to us?"

"I know the answer to that one. Cats have always believed that if other people can't be bothered to learn to understand cat-speak, then it's their own problem. Her universal translator implant isn't set to speak the local language like ours. It'll help her to understand what the natives say, but she's still speaking cat."

"So with our implants, we're the only ones who can understand her?"

---

[1]Weaving a kind of coarse material from bast, the fibrous inner bark of a tree.

"That's it. As far as everyone else is concerned, she's just a big moggy that mewls, purrs and growls a lot."

Betel grinned. "Now I know why old Chive didn't give her a sleeping cubicle. I'll bet she's really cheesed off about that!"

The Magician grinned too. "Actually," he said, "it must be rough on her. After all, the Princess probably isn't used to being ignored."

"Princess," said Betel, "that's about right. Every cat I've ever met has behaved like some sort of royalty."

"No, you don't understand. She really is a princess. She was travelling back to her home planet after a diplomatic tour of the Federation's seventeen feline worlds. I don't know whether Yellow Star Lines would spend much time or trouble searching for three lost entertainers, but I'll tell you this, ... they'll tear this solar system apart to find the Princess Mrouwl!"

"Great! So my best chance of being rescued from this primitive mud-ball is to stay really close to twenty kilos of walking fur coat with an attitude?"

"That's it!" The Magician yawned. "I think I'll turn in. See you in the morning."

"Goodnight," said Betel and he was instantly asleep.

Chive was also preparing to go to bed. He went out and checked that the animals were all safe in their pens. He banked up the fire so that it would burn slowly through the night, and last of all he put down a saucer of cream for the hearthsprite[1]. The house was already filled with the sounds of his sleeping guests as he lay down on his wicker bed and pulled the blanket over his face.

The cat was dozing by the fire. She sniffed and opened one eye. Maybe the folk here weren't so uncaring after all, someone appeared

---

[1]An unwelcome but inevitable lodger in every home, the hearthsprite (sometimes also called a hobgoblin) had to be placated with gifts of cream and fresh-baked cakes or it would wreak havoc by playing mischievous tricks on all the inhabitants of the house. Nothing could ever persuade it to venture out of doors, where it felt exposed and threatened.

to have left her a little snack! Full of cream she gave her face a wash and settled down comfortably for a little nap.

The hearthsprite was livid! Never in the many generations that it had lived amongst the humans had it been so outrageously treated! The creature that had stolen its cream would suffer for its perfidy, or the sprite's name was not Gewindgwy[1].

Confident in its invisibility to mortal eyes, the creature tip-toed soundlessly up to the drowsing cat, its intention to pull out the beast's whiskers one at a time.

Cats are magical creatures who can see things that human eyes are blind to. Any cat owner will tell you how Trixie (or Whiskers, or Smudge) will suddenly rouse and stare in fascination at something that no-one else in the house can see.

Mrouwl watched through half-closed eyes as the tiny figure approached. Thirty centimetres tall and dressed in ragged brown clothes, it crept closer, knees and elbows sticking out, long taloned fingers spread. It was standing between her paws when she sprang to her feet, hair erect and hissed at it with all the force of a geothermal geyser.

The goblin screamed and covered its eyes, rather like an ostrich seeking invisibility through its own blindness. Slowly, very slowly, it spread its fingers and peered between them. The cat grinned at it, displaying rows of needle sharp teeth and a tongue rough enough to lick the paint off a door.

"Aaaaaaaaargh!" The goblin ran pell mell through the house and out into the night, pausing only to grab its bag and scarlet cap from their place by the hearth.

The cat yawned, stretched, and went to look for somewhere more comfortable to sleep for the rest of the night.

---

[1]Not that he would ever admit that it was his name, since to possess anyone's true name is to have magical power over that person. That's why the Herbert at the Town Hall who's led you such a dance over the 'phone about the taxable value of your property won't ever identify himself.

In the small hours of the morning, Bryony was awakened by an unfamiliar presence in her bed. A pair of amber eyes regarded her for a moment and then they were covered by a long and delightfully fluffy tail. The rumbling vibration that the creature was making was very relaxing and in a few moments Bryony drifted back into deep and untroubled sleep.

Chapter 8

The next morning came much too soon. The light of day didn't really penetrate far into the roundhouse, but the bustle of folk going about their business, coupled with the cries of the livestock, made sleep difficult for anyone who was used to the insulated silence of a cabin on board a luxury liner.

The Magician knuckled the sleep from his eyes and lifted himself onto one elbow. The straw filled pallet had proved more comfortable than he'd expected and he had slept soundly.

"Good morning," said Bryony, handing him a mug of something sweet and milky. "You'd better get up quickly or your friend will have finished all the porridge."

Betel was sitting by the fire, helping himself to another serving of the porridge which was keeping warm in a large pot on the hearth. "You should try some of this," he said, "it's very good."

"I've never been a big fan of porridge, a bit of toast will be fine."

"Toast?" Bryony looked puzzled. "What is toast?"

"A slice of bread," explained the Magician, "stale bread is fine. You brown it in front of the fire and spread it with butter."

"I'm sorry," Bryony looked genuinely unhappy. "We make our bread fresh every day. Any left overs go to the animals. There'll be bread with our evening meal."

"No, it's me who ought to be sorry. I forgot for a moment that you'd have different ways of doing things. I'll have a bowl of that porridge thank you, if Betel hasn't eaten it all."

The Magician had been wrong when he assumed that the villagers were not curious about their visitors. Throughout the morning there was a constant coming and going as neighbours dropped in to say hello and look the strangers over. By midday they were both exhausted. Everybody asked what they did. Nobody seemed to understand when the two friends explained that they were entertainers. Betel wondered whether the translator implant was doing its job properly. The Magician decided that a demonstration was going to save a lot of explaining.

By late afternoon most of the people had gathered outside Chive's house. Betel was the warm up man walking round amongst the crowd juggling a variety of small objects. There were oohs and aahs as three eggs spun above his head, and gasps as he pretended that he was about to drop them. The climax of his act was to juggle three totally dissimilar objects while balancing on a plank that was in turn resting across one of Chive's small barrels. He leapt down to delighted applause, neatly catching the stool, the clay pot and the ladle in his hands and took a bow. This was without doubt the best audience he'd ever performed for!

"And now, ladies and gentlemen, I should like to demonstrate for you some of the legerdemain that has baffled the very Princes of the Universe!" The Magician, resplendent in his freshly sponged tail coat and top hat, emerged from the doorway of Chive's house. It was not the entrance he had intended. The children took one look at his outlandish clothes and burst into peals of laughter.

"Behold, ladies and gentlemen, this perfectly ordinary billiard ball." He held it up for everyone to see. "Now you see it," he rotated his hand, "now you don't!" He paused for reaction from the audience. Not a sausage!

"Where can it have gone?" He strode quickly across to a small boy and reached behind the urchin's ear. "Voila!" In his hand were two billiard balls. He hardly noticed the lack of applause. Two? Something was wrong.

"Bryony my dear, I have something for you from Betel." He reached into his jacket and withdrew an impossibly large bunch of flowers. No, two bunches! What the heck was happening? The audience seemed pretty unimpressed. If he didn't know better, he would have sworn that they'd seen it all before.

He took three sheets of coloured paper from his pocket and rapidly tore them up. "I roll the pieces into a ball, like so, and I pop it into my mouth." He rolled the rice paper around in his mouth for a few moments and then ostentatiously reached inside with his fingers and withdrew TWO strings of flags!

There was a sprinkling of polite applause and the crowd began to disperse.

"I don't understand it," he told Chive as they sat beside the fire after their evening meal. No-one seemed even slightly impressed by any of my magic."

"Well, sir," said Chive slowly, obviously trying not to give offence, "people hereabouts see quite a bit of magic, living so near to the seminary and all. One or two in the village can do a little bit themselves. Them as has the talent. I think you'd need to do sommat a bit more spectaklar to get these folk excited. Now that friend of yours, he's a rare treat though, ain't he?"

"Yes," said the Magician absently, "he's very clever."

Later on Betel confused the Magician even more. "It seems that everybody believes that magic is for real," he reported. "They say that if you have the talent, all you have to do is believe that it's going to happen, and it does."

"All you have to do is believe?"

"That's right," said Betel. "Believing is the tricky bit though. Apparently, some wizards even use alcohol and drugs[1] to help them overcome their doubts! You can stop someone else's magic working too - if you disbelieve strongly enough."

"Nonsense," his friend was not going to accept the existence of real magic. "I've been in the trade all my working life. There's no such thing as magic. It's all trickery and sleight of hand."

"Say what you like," Betel persisted, "but it would explain what happened to your act this afternoon. You believed there would be a red

[1]A dangerous practice since the monsters inspired by drunkenness can assume corporeal form! Ten years previously, after his sister's wedding, the famed Wizard-priest Caleb the Calamitous had found himself sitting on the doorstep in the small hours of the morning holding an animated conversation with a large pink aurochs. He later lapsed into unconsciousness, and the aurochs, thus freed from the dubious control of his pickled brain, galloped off and destroyed twelve dwellings before a group of Caleb's more sober peers managed to corner it in the potter's house and disbelieve it back into oblivion.

ball in your hand, and so there was - a magical one - in addition to the one you conjured there in the usual way."

"That's a very neat explanation," admitted the Magician, "except for one thing. There is quite definitely no such thing as magic!"

He went off to his cubicle and spent the next thirty minutes going through the pockets of his conjuror's suit, making sure that he knew exactly what was in there.

The magician wasn't the only person who had searched those pockets on that summer's day. Earlier on, before he was even awake, his new friend Betel had rummaged through his jacket. It wasn't that Betel was dishonest. It wasn't even that he was interested in conjuring. All that Betel had wanted to know was the real name of the jacket's owner.

There were a great many things hidden away in that jacket. There were packs of cards. There were silk handkerchiefs and flags. There were several different magic wands and numerous pieces of rope and cord. There was a place for a pair of white doves, although they didn't seem to be home at the moment and there were several ingeniously devised bunches of flowers that folded down to almost nothing if you knew the secret.

Betel didn't know the secret. It took him twenty panic stricken minutes to fold down a bunch of flowers and replace it in its secret pocket. "Make a note," he told himself. "If you want to know a magician's real name - don't look in his jacket!"

Later that evening Betel tried the direct approach. He took a sip of his hot milk and leaned back. "Can I ask you a personal question?"

"Of course you can," said the Magician. "What is it?"

"Ever since I first met you, I've only ever thought of you as *the Magician*. That's no kind of name for a friend. Haven't you got a real name?"

"It's the only name I ever use," the Magician replied. "What would you like to call me?"

In the middle of the fire a log slipped and a galaxy of sparks spiralled upwards towards the shiny blackened timbers of the roof. In one compartment of his mind, Betel watched the sparks fly and thought how curious it was that they always went out before they reached the thatch. He dragged his mind back to the conversation. "What do your other friends call you?"

"I don't have many real friends. Just Gloria, and of course, you Betel."

"All right then," Betel said, still probing. "What did your parents call you?"

"I didn't spend much time with them really. As soon as I was old enough to carry a small suitcase they sent me off to boarding school. On the odd occasions I can remember being with them, I recall they called me ... *The*."

"Your parents called you *Thuh*?" Betel began to think that he was being made the butt of a joke.

"No, not *Thuh* - make the *ee* sound longer, *The*."

"O.K .," said Betel. "Fine! I'm sorry I asked! Why didn't you just tell me to mind my own business?"

"I'm not poking fun at you Betel," the Magician wasn't laughing. "Nor am I offended. I really haven't used any other name for a long long time and my parents really did call me *The*. I'd be glad to have you call me that too. Gloria's the only other living person who does, now that Mum and Dad are gone."

"Thanks!" Betel was grateful that his companion thought of him as a real friend. He'd lived a solitary life and he valued the Magician's affection more than he could ever admit. He finished off his milk and lay back on his pallet. "Goodnight - *The*."

"Goodnight my friend."

Chapter 9

"Hallo Uncle Grog!" Bryony was giving her new-found friends the grand tour. "This is Betel and his friend is called the Magician."

Grog nodded in their direction. "Saw yer jugglin' yesterday lad. I ain't never seen nothin' like it afore. Where'd yer learn that stuff?"

Betel stood a little taller. "Self taught mostly," he said. "But I had an uncle who worked in a circus and he spent some time teaching us kids when he retired."

"My youngest lad, Pug, he were right taken wi' all that jugglin' stuff. He's bin throwin' stuff inter the air ever since. He even catches some of it on the way down. The missus reckons he's got a flair fer it. Might it be that yer could spare some time ter give 'im some pointers?"

"Spare time's not something we're short of at the moment. We haven't worked out how we can be useful yet. So, I'd be happy to, only...."

"Go on."

".... some people don't have the talent. If he turns out not to be a natural, I'd have to be honest and tell you, you understand?"

"I'd expect nuthin' else. And by way of exchange, ... if yer fancy learnin' ter make yer own pots, I'd be glad ter give yer some lessons."

"Why thank you!" Betel had been thinking how fascinating the workshop looked. He'd love to know how a pile of clay could be transformed into the beautifully decorated pots that everyone in the village used.

Grog extended a hand. "It's a deal then?"

"It's a deal."

As they walked across the compound, the Magician told Betel how fortunate he thought he was. "I'm not good with my hands," he said, " so I don't know how I'm going to fit into this society. I don't think I could make pots, or weave baskets and as for making barrels like Chive ..."

Betel's face lit up. "I think I've got the answer," he grinned. "You've worked for years with doves and ...... whatchamacallits? Lagomorpha! You must be good with animals!"

"Betel, you're a genius! Why didn't I think of that? I've always loved animals. Bryony? Who looks after the animals?"

An hour later, it seemed to poor Betel that the two friends had looked at a host of animals. The cattle were short-legged, black and large-eyed. Their tails were long enough to drag on the ground. One of them had decided that Betel's shirt looked tasty and had chewed it thoroughly before his friend had rescued him.

Whilst inspecting the pig sties Betel had made the mistake of stroking the largest sow. Grateful for this unusual attention, the sow had leaned affectionately against him, pinning him immovably against the wall of the sty. It had taken the combined efforts of three strong men to part the creature from her new-found friend.

Easily the biggest disaster were the sheep. "Sheep are easily controlled," explained the Magician, "because they always stick together in bunches."

Are you sure about that?" asked an already wary Betel nervously, "I mean, how can you be certain?"

"Did you ever do collective nouns at school?"

"Collective what?"

"Nouns! You know, like a *herd* of cows or a *gaggle* of geese ..... ?"

"Oh, I see! You mean like a *round* of drinks?"

"Er, yes ..... sort of. Well, what's the collective noun for a lot of sheep then?"

Betel, whose upbringing had been in a high-tech mining settlement on a hostile planet, thought hard. "It's er, don't tell me, it's er, er, a FLOCK .... right?"

"Right! And why is it a flock? Don't worry, I'll tell you - it's 'cos sheep always flock together! Did you ever hear anyone talk about a *scatter* of sheep?"

"No," said Betel thoughtfully. "I never did."

"They're just like the sheep we have at home[1]," explained the Magician, gazing fondly at the small, lightly built and rather skittish brown animals. He stepped easily over the low fence of wicker hurdles and moved towards a ewe, making soothing noises. The ewe let out a bleat of terror and leapt vertically a metre and a half in the air. For a moment the magician was surrounded by a bucking crowd of panic stricken animals and then, almost with one accord, they leapt over the fence and scattered toward every point of the compass[2].

Twenty minutes later the two friends collapsed on a fallen log and fought to regain their breath. The Magician rubbed ineffectually at a mossy smear on his trousers, picked up when trying to rugby-tackle one of the remarkably individualistic sheep which were still spreading out all over the forest. Betel smiled. "I think we've finally found a job for you," he said.

"Oh?"

"Yes, I reckon it's going to take you the rest of your life to get that lot back into their pen!"

Their conversation was interrupted by the distant ringing of a bell. "What's that?" Betel asked.

"Dunno. Perhaps there's trouble at the village?"

A scruffy brown ewe with twigs in its fleece trotted past them on its way back to the settlement. Another one followed. The two friends watched in disbelief as the whole flock filed docilely back home.

Perhaps we'd better follow them?" suggested the Magician sheepishly.

---

[1]The theory of convergent evolution says that on planets sharing similar conditions, plants and animals will tend to evolve toward amazingly similar end products. Amongst other things, this means that every Earth-like planet in the universe has dog excrement all over its pavements.

[2]There's an exception to every rule.

Chapter 10

The land around here had once been covered by a dense layer of forest. The trees were mostly deciduous and many of them took several lifetimes to grow to maturity. In the past, farming methods had been primitive. Slashing and burning cleared fresh, fertile plots which were planted and harvested until they were exhausted. The land had not been cared for because new plots were so easy to clear.

Now the situation was different. Farmers were learning to tend the soil, fertilizing it and rotating their crops. Much of the old forest was gone, except for isolated patches growing on the least accessible hillsides. New trees were often prevented from growing to maturity by the pigs which grubbed up their roots. However, not all of the historic woodland had been destroyed. Not far from the village was a wide belt of ancient weald, dark, secret and foreboding.

The cat was deep in the forest. All afternoon she'd had that funny itchy feeling that cats get at the back of the neck when someone is watching them[1]. Yet every time she turned around, there was no-one to be seen. If anything was shadowing her, it was staying out of sight and was probably more afraid of her than she was of it. Apart from this one strange irritant there seemed to be nothing in these woods that posed any threat to her at all. She had met some sort of dog with a reddish coat and a bushy tail that was large enough to be a threat to the local wildcats, but it had taken one look at her and decided that discretion was the better part of Vulpes.

You wouldn't have thought that golden fur would be very effective as woodland camouflage, but the cat was mistress of the art of blending into her surroundings. Her colouring actually worked very well in the dappled sunlight and she had surprised more than one native of these woods today. The local wildcat couldn't believe it when she rose out of the undergrowth right in front of him. Princess Mrouwl was pleased to discover that the local cat speak was much like other primitive

---

[1]Humans get that feeling too, but because we don't believe in our sixth sense we ignore the warnings it tries to give us. In the end it gives up and abandons us to our own devices. That's why muggers are so successful.

feline languages but disappointed by the limited vocabulary. She suspected that it reflected a limited mentality.

"What you?"

Mrouwl sat down and licked a paw. "I am the Princess Mrouwl. What is your name?"

"Der, what you?"

"Take a look sonny. I'm the kind of cat you could be ..... given a few hundreds of thousands of years of uninterrupted evolution."

"Der, you ...... cat?"

"Yes, I'm a cat. So you can put all that ruffled hair down and stop trying to look bigger than you really are. I probably outmass you by more than two to one and I have a black collar in Kung Fur."

The wildcat tried to work out what to do next. His limited repertoire held only two strategies for dealing with other cats. You either saw them off your territory or you mated with them. In his experience female cats turned nasty immediately after mating and this one looked like a real handful. In any case, he hadn't brought a step ladder. That left only one alternative.

"Der, dis my place!"

"Oh, it's to be the territorial imperative is it? All right then, get on with it."

"Wot? Oh! Er, you go now, or you sorry!"

"Oh good grief, this is so primitive. Very well then, if that's the way you want it." Mrouwl stood up and erected all of her fur. It made her look enormous. Her eyes narrowed and her ears flattened themselves against her skull. Her lips slid back, exposing rows of needle sharp teeth in a mouth that looked large enough to engulf his entire head. She hissed with all the force of an antique steam engine.

"Dere again, not rush dis. Room for both! Us friends?"

"Yes, yes, us friends. Now get up. You look so pathetic on your back with your paws in the air."

The Princess was soon alone again. Her new found friend seemed nervous in her presence and before long he bounded off to investigate some sound or scent in the far distance. He didn't come back. As she strolled off in the direction of the village, the golden-furred alien reflected that she was unlikely to find any companionship among the cats of this world.

The woods were teeming with wildlife and it occurred to her that a small offering might go down rather well upon her return. The fat pigeon didn't see her coming and never knew what hit it.

"Mama!"

Mrouwl put one paw on her contribution to the evening meal and pricked up her ears.

"Mama!"

Cautiously slipping into a small clearing, her body pressed close to the ground and all her senses at full stretch, she became aware of a body at the foot of a tree. It was a female adult wildcat, badly savaged and quite dead. Judging by the blood and hair on its claws and muzzle, the other participant in the fight was in a sorry state too.

"Mama!" A stripy grey and black head with enormous ears emerged from the fur. The kitten ignored Mrouwl and began to lick the face of what must have been its mother. "Mama!"

Mrouwl's voice was a gentle rumble. "Are you hungry?"

"Hungry!"

"Then perhaps you'd better come along with me. I know where there's a nice plump pigeon that we can share. Besides, whatever did that to your mother might come back. I think you'd be safer away from here."

An hour later, the Princess padded into Chive's hut carrying a sleepy kitten by the scruff of its neck. She put it down gently by the fire and spoke to it soothingly. "Don't be afraid. These are my friends. They won't hurt you. O.K?"

"Mama!"

"I'm not your Mama. You can call me Mrouwl. Now go to sleep."

"Sleepy Mama!"

"Just go to sleep."

Chapter 11

The middle of the day was an odd time to be taking a bath, but the Magician still hadn't come to terms with the villagers' easy going attitude towards nakedness. Chive was delivering some barrels to a merchant across the valley and Bryony had gone off gathering berries for a special treat tonight. Even the Princess had taken the kitten off in search of small game to hunt and so he was quite alone except for Betel who was struggling to bind some staves together with strips of hazel to make a wooden bucket. Betel was trying hard to learn some of the skills that Chive made his living from, and he was showing a good deal of promise, judging by his teacher's lavish praise.

The Magician was sitting in what looked like half of a beer barrel. It was part filled with rapidly cooling water and he was trying with only partial success to rinse away the foul mixture of animal grease and ashes that memory had told him was the way to make soap.

"You want this after me?" he queried.

Betel grimaced. "I wouldn't rub myself with that stuff if you paid me," he said. "I'd rather be dirty."

"You <u>are</u> dirty," his friend told him with a smile. "Still, I know what you mean. Also, this might be the biggest tub that Chive has ever made, but it's still pretty uncomfortable." He didn't look like someone enjoying a relaxing soak. His knees were under his chin and his toes were cramped painfully against the side of the tub.

"I know what we need," he said. "We need .... ," his eyes glazed as he looked into a possible future. "Eureka!"

"I know," said Betel, affronted. "You already told me so."

"No! It means something like, I've got it!" He leapt out of the tub and began throwing on his clothes. "Come on Betel," he shouted, "this is going to be fun."

As they walked along the path of the stream, the Magician began to explain. "We need to find a place where the banks of the stream are quite steep. Then we need lots of big stones." In just a few minutes they came to the ideal spot. The stream was flowing downhill through steep stony banks.

Both men set to carrying the largest stones they could handle and placing them in a rough wall across the bed of the stream. As the dam grew taller it needed to be thickened to resist the pressure of the water building up behind it. It took three hours to raise a dam high enough to create a pool about a metre deep.

"This is more like it," sighed the Magician as he floated lazily on his back, watching a lone bird of prey hover overhead.

Betel never had been able to float. As soon as he stretched out, his legs sank. He was just lying back in the water, absently scratching his back against the stones of the dam wall. Suddenly he ducked down under the water until only his head was showing. "Oh good grief!" he muttered.

"What's the matter?"

Betel looked across at his friend who was still staring up at the sky. He had obviously been thinking about Gloria.

"Hide yourself," Betel hissed, "there's somebody coming!"

"Hello boys." Bryony must have had a good afternoon. The basket was full and her face was smeared with purple juice from the berries she had eaten. The Magician folded in the middle and went under in a welter of bubbles and thrashing limbs.

"What a wonderful idea!" Bryony seemed oblivious to the two fiery red faces and the strategically cupped hands below the water line. "I think I'll join you!" She dropped her basket and in one fluid movement pulled her woollen dress over her head.

Betel was transfixed. He thought that he had never seen anything so beautiful in his entire life. Even his love lorn companion might have forgiven him for saying so. His eyes caressed the firm young curves of her breasts and travelled lovingly down past her amazingly slim waist and slightly rounded tummy to the triangular mass of curling chestnut hair that concealed her ......

Betel's knees began to give way. He closed his eyes tightly and concentrated on not trembling.

Bryony entered the pool in an explosion of water droplets. She playfully dashed a double handful of water into Betel's face. "Come on Betel," she laughed, "let's have a water fight!"

Without thinking, Betel lifted both hands to his face to wipe the water out of his eyes. As his blurred vision returned he saw that Bryony was looking down with an impish smile.

"Oh Betel," she giggled, "you're standing up for me. How sweet! And what a big boy you are!" She leaned forward and kissed him.

Betel barely had time to register the warm softness of her lips and the gentle touch of her breast against his arm before she was gone, climbing gracefully out of the pool and slipping back into her dress.

"Hurry home boys," she shouted, "or there won't be any fruit and cream left for you."

Suddenly she was gone. The place seemed empty without her.

"Betel," said the Magician thoughtfully, "you're a very lucky man!"

"Lucky?" Betel croaked. It crossed his mind that his throat shouldn't be so dry when he was immersed in thousands of litres of fresh water.

"She's in love with you. Surely you can tell?"

"*The*," said his friend hopelessly, "you're out of your mind. She's the most beautiful creature in the universe. She can choose any man on this planet, and unless he's certifiably insane he'll be her slave and spend the rest of his life in a delirium of happiness. So why would she choose a scrawny red-nosed comic, juggler and monocyclist with no social graces and no skills worth mentioning outside of a circus?"

"Beats the hell out of me," agreed the Magician, "but I could see it in her face. You would have too, if your lascivious eyes had been able to overcome the force of gravity."

Betel blushed again. "I sort of lost control of my eyes," he admitted. "When my brain called them up, it kept getting the engaged tone."

"You really don't get it, do you? She wanted you to look. She's telling you that she's interested. She's saying, 'Look, all this can be yours.' Tell her how you feel about her, Betel, and I guarantee that she'll fall into your arms."

“I don’t know,” Betel murmured, “I don’t think I’m brave enough to tell her how I feel. If she were to laugh at me, I’d break into tiny pieces.”

The Magician smiled. “I’m a poor adviser,” he said. “Just before the accident, I was lying on my bunk talking to the ceiling, because I couldn’t find the courage to talk to Gloria. Let’s get back to the village.”

Betel smiled sympathetically. “Perhaps we’ll both be able to tell them how we feel - one day.”

Chapter 12

Meanwhile, just beyond the village of Muddybrook, Gloria's education was proceeding apace. Old Meg had taken her out to gather food and herbs. They had stuffed a bag with leaves from two kinds of trees. The leaves of one were heart-shaped and pale green in colour, the others were smaller and darker. "These are both good in a salad," Meg told her, "or you can cook them in hot water and serve them as a vegetable with roast meat."

"These are useful," Meg went on, pointing to a large clump of tall dark green plants with serrated leaves and no obvious flowers. "No! Don't ....." It was too late. Gloria had taken a handful. Her hand prickled and burned. The irritation extended some way up her forearm.

"We call them stingers," Meg told her. "The stems give a fibre that can be woven. The leaves can be cooked and eaten, or used to clean your hair. Next time, wrap a cloth around your hand before you pick them."

In the woods they found two delicacies. The first was a feathery umbellifer which grew amongst the Wood blues. It had a pea-sized tuber and Meg called it a Root-nut. The second was a plant with a three angled stem. Its leaves were broad and pointed with parallel veins. Beneath the soil was a small narrow bulb. "Bruise it," Meg instructed her.

Gloria rubbed a little of the skin off the bulb with her thumb and the air was immediately full of a sharp sulphurous odour. "This smells like something we have at home," she said. "We use it to flavour stews and cheeses."

Old Meg smiled. "So do we."

In the shade of some scrubby bushes they found a few tall hairy plants, rather like stingers, but with reddish whorls of flowers and four angled stems. "These are called Staunch-blood," said Meg. "They stop wounds bleeding and help them to heal without festering."

A little further on they sat down on a fallen tree trunk and munched thick slices of bread topped with cheese. Gloria scattered a few crumbs and watched to see which birds would be brave enough to come and peck them up. “I love this place,” she said. “It’s a lot like my home in many ways, but quieter and more peaceful.” Her voice took on a wistful tone. “I wish *The* could have come here with me.”

Her new friend moved a little closer. “Tell me about him,” she said.

“He was a very gentle man,” Gloria told her. “He didn’t share his feelings easily and didn’t make many close friendships. I think that deep inside he was afraid of being hurt. I know he loved me, but somehow he could never find a way to tell me so, and I never found a way to help him. I used to dream of giving up our travelling life and settling down together in a place something like this.

“I thought you said he was a Wizard?” Meg seemed a little surprised.

“Well,” said Gloria, “sort of.”

“Didn’t you know? Wizards never settle down and live happily ever after. It’s an all male affair is wizarding. They reckon that women cancel out a man’s ability to work magic.[1] As if we couldn’t do all the magic that they do, if we wanted to. But we prefer the natural ways. The fact is, they’ve never heard of working in harmony with nature. It’s all conflict and aggression. They have to make the whole world change to suit them. They don’t work with the Mother Goddess the way that we do.”

Gloria shook her head. “He wasn’t that kind of wizard,” she argued. “He wasn’t married to his magic, just trapped by it. I don’t think he was even enjoying the life he was leading. I’m sure we could have been happy together.”

“So where is he now? Did he go off and leave you?”

“Oh, no,” Gloria’s eyes were moist. “There was a terrible accident. He made me take the only way of escape, and stayed behind. He must have died.”

Meg shot a look of pure amazement at her. “You mean you haven’t checked?”

---

[1]When asked if anything was worn under the robes, Wizard-priests invariably replied, “No, because it’s never been used!”

"Checked?" Gloria was out of her depth. "What do you mean, checked?"

"Come on," said Meg, grabbing Gloria's hand. We're going back to my place."

Back at Meg's house, the fire had burned low. They fed it with sticks until it was flickering brightly again. Meg brought out a shallow bronze bowl and set Gloria to burnishing it with sand until it gleamed. Into a second bowl, the older woman put some coals from the fire. She blew on them until they glowed.

"Now," she said, "for this magic to work, we must both be as the Mother made us. Take off your clothes."

The two women sat down cross legged and sky clad on opposite sides of the shining dish. Meg filled it to the brim with clear water and then she threw a handful of dried leaves onto the hot coals. Instantly the house was filled with a fragrant smoke.

"We should sing. Do you have a favourite song, Gloria?"

Gloria thought for a moment. "There is one song," she admitted. "It was his favourite." She turned her eyes inward as if searching, then took a deep breath and began to sing in a clear, melodious voice.

“When we awake,
Dreams start to fade,
Their colours and their forms,
Of gossamer are made.

Yet dreams define
Just who we are,
In life’s long lonely night,
A tiny flickering star.

We are unique,
None else the same,
Defined by fleeting dreams,
And not by given name.

Remember dreams,
Past morning’s light,
For if your dreams survive,
Then everything’s alright.”

Gloria felt very much at peace. Opposite her Meg was crooning the melody again and again. She realized that she was beginning to doze. “It must be something in that smoke,” she thought.

She forced her eyes open. In the bowl of water she could see the reflection of her face. As she looked at the reflection, it began to change. Slowly the face lengthened. The hair darkened and grew shorter. A moustache appeared. It dawned on her that she was looking at the face of her beloved Magician. He was lying on his back, floating in a pool of some sort and she could tell that he was thinking of her.

Gloria smiled a happy smile. He was alive after all. She reached out to touch him. As her fingers brushed against the bowl the water rippled and the vision was gone. Her eyes began to close again and her head sank forward. Gloria slept peacefully.

Chapter 13

The Magician was bone weary. Working in the fields was a new experience, and whilst he was more than willing to contribute his full share to the work of the household, his muscles didn't yet have the staying power of his resolve. He leaned back against a pile of fleeces and stretched his legs in front of the fire.

He was sure that the evening meal had been delicious - Bryony's cooking always was, but he realized with some surprise that he couldn't remember eating it.

" ...... sure you'll get on like an 'ouse on fire."

"I'm sorry Chive, I was miles away. What were you saying?"

"I were tellin' you about old Biddy. She knows everyone round these parts. Brought most of us inter the world an' all. She'll be here any time now."

"I'm afraid I'd be very poor company tonight. I think it might be best if I just crept off to bed and left you to it. Perhaps we could have a little chat some other time?"

Chive looked horrified. "But you can't do that - 'tis you she's come to see. She'll have a little proposition for you if I don't miss my guess."

The Magician turned to Betel and groaned. "A little proposition?" he queried. "If there was one thing that I really liked about this world more than anything else, it was my belief in the total and absolute absence of door to door insurance salesmen!"

"I don't think she's an insurance salesperson," said Betel thoughtfully.

"She's not coming to sell you anything," agreed Bryony, "but I expect she'll be bringing someone with her."

"Oh no." In his current state of exhaustion, the Magician's brain was playing out one disastrous scenario after another. "We have those back on my home world. They always travel in pairs. You answer the door and it's wedged open by a size eleven shoe. Then a voice with a crewcut gabbles,
'GoodeveningwearethemessengersofGodandwecometobringyouGod's

message - maywecomein?' and the next thing you know they're sitting on the sofa in the lounge and you're still in the hall examining the ceiling tiles and trying to work out how they got past you without leaving footprints on them."

Suddenly the sound of doom penetrated the wattle and daub of the hut's outside wall. "Coo - ee! Is anybody home?"

"Come in Biddy," Chive began to rush about, fetching her something to sit on, taking her stick and generally fussing. "Bryony, what about making another beaker of tea?"

Biddy was a short woman in late middle age. Her almost spherical frame was draped in a welter of skirts and shawls so that she seemed to have more layers than an onion. She sat down on one of Chive's upturned baskets and shrugged her shawls into place like a chicken settling her feathers.

She looked around, her sharp little eyes taking everything in. "You must be the one they call the Magician," she said. "This is Ivy. Her father is the smith over at Barrowfield."

Her companion was a tall big-boned girl who somehow gave the impression of being all knees ands elbows. She had reddish hair and her cheeks were a mass of rioting freckles.

"Pleased to meet you Ivy," said the Magician dutifully.

The kitten came in at a gallop. In the couple of days since arriving in the village he had become incredibly confident. The house belonged to him and he treated everyone else as a lodger. He shot through the gap that had been left for him in the door, skidded around the fire and leapt into the air. He hit Biddy square in the chest with all four paws and fell, apparently already fast asleep, onto her lap. It was his favourite trick and it had already reduced one or two of the more nervous neighbours to hysterics.

Biddy didn't turn a hair. She coo'd and tickled the furry bandit under the chin. "Who's a little sweetie then?" He purred frantically and wriggled with pleasure.

Princess Mrouwl looked up from her spot near the hearth and growled. "Oh yes," she grumbled, "he's a little sweetie alright. That's his trouble. Look at him - the pinnacle of feline evolution on this dreadful planet - curled up in a human lap begging for affection. He hasn't got a scrap of dignity!"

"Don't be so hard on him," Biddy smiled. "He's only a baby and he's got a lot of learning to do. He'll be a fine cat one day."

The Princess stared at her with wide eyes. "You can understand me?"

"A little. I can understand most creatures, but your speech is more difficult than most. You're not from round here, are you?"

"No," allowed the cat, "I'm from - a long way away, further than you can imagine."

"You shouldn't underestimate the power of imagination." Biddy somehow didn't look like a woman whose mental horizons were limited. "I'd like a long chat with you one day, if you'd permit it."

"I should enjoy that." To her surprise, the Princess realised that she wasn't just being polite.

"Tea's ready," said Bryony brightly. "Would you like honey in it Aunty Biddy?"

"I shouldn't really, but I do like a little in my tea - don't you dear? I know it's bad for the teeth, but I love sweet things. Ivy doesn't have honey in her tea and she's got excellent teeth. Don't you think Ivy's got excellent teeth Mr Magician?"

It was true. Ivy did have remarkable teeth. Comparing them to ordinary teeth was like comparing Buckingham Palace to a bungalow. They were heroic teeth. Ivy's upper lip had long ago given up the unequal struggle and no longer even tried to cover them. They were perpetually displayed in all their considerable glory.

"My Dad thays my teeth are my betht feature," she lisped.

"They are - impressive," admitted the Magician, feeling rather baffled by the evening's events.

"Have one of these biscuits," offered Biddy, rummaging in her bag. "Ivy made them herself. She's a fine cook is Ivy!" She elbowed the Magician in the ribs and winked conspiratorially. A worried expression flitted across his face, looked around, decided it could be comfortable here and settled down for an extended visit.

He coughed nervously and got to his feet. “I’m d-dreadfully sorry,” he stammered. I’ve just remembered that I promised to help Betel perfect a gag before bedtime. If you’ll just excuse us ladies, we’ll be back in no time at all. Come on Betel.” He grabbed his friend by the sleeve and dragged him bodily from the roundhouse, ignoring the ensuing chorus of disappointed female cries.

“For crying out loud!” he hissed, the moment they were outside. “What the blazes is going on in there?”

"Weeeell," Betel was torn between honesty and the need to spare his friend’s feelings. “I think that little round spinster is the local witch.”

“I’d worked that out for myself.”

“And one of the jobs that witches get to do round here,” Betel ignored the interruption, “is marriage broking.”

“But I don’t want to get married! At least, I do want to get married, but I don’t want to get married <u>off</u>! I don’t need any help. I can do it all by myself! Why has Chive encouraged that dreadful little woman to pick on me?”

“Look around you *The*. In this society when a young man marries he brings the girl into the extended family. The grandparents help care for the kiddies and the youngsters look after the old folk in their declining years. Old Chive hasn’t got any sons at all. If Bryony were to marry and leave he’d be all alone in his old age. He’s hoping that you’ll marry and bring the girl into his home. It would strengthen the family unit.”

“Fine! If it’s that important to him, he can come and live with Gloria and me when we set up house. He knows I’m going to marry Gloria.”

“He’s heard you say so often enough. But he’s never seen Gloria. I think he doubts that she even exists. And round here most young men are married by the age of fifteen. You’re an old man by their standards. He probably thinks that you’ll die childless without a bit of help.”

The Magician grimaced. “O.K. so his intentions are good. But his taste is dreadful. Have you looked at that Ivy? She’s got more enamel than a luxury bathroom suite!” He rummaged in his pocket and took out the biscuit. He nibbled it thoughtfully. “You know, this isn’t bad!”

Betel shuddered. “Good grief! You’ve already complemented her on her impressive dental equipment. Go back in there and tell her you like her biscuits and they’ll be setting the wedding day!”

The Magician stared at the offending confection in horror. He looked around, spotted one of the village dogs sniffing around the woodpile and threw it a snack. Don’t ever let anyone tell you that dog’s faces can’t register emotion. This dog looked flabbergasted. No-one had ever given it food before - at least, not voluntarily. It sniffed suspiciously at the biscuit before gobbling it down.

“Come on,” said Betel. “Let’s get back in there and see if we can find a diplomatic way out of this. And remember, no more compliments!”

Inside the house the conversation had turned to babies. “Of course,” said Biddy, “Ivy here is the oldest of thirteen children. She’s had lots of experience with little ones. She’ll make an excellent mother! Do you like children Mr Magician?”

“Oh! Er - children?” The Magician tried to think of a response that wouldn’t get him into trouble. “You mean - er - little ones ..... um?”

At that moment the kitten, which had been getting restive for some minutes since it was no longer being stroked, decided to try for a different lap. It stood up, stretched, yawned and gathered itself before taking a flying leap onto Ivy’s knee.

Ivy squealed and flapped a hand at it ineffectually. The kitten interpreted this as an invitation to play and grabbing the hand with its front paws began to chew her thumb whilst raking her wrist with the claws of its back feet.

Ivy’s cries grew more urgent. She leapt to her feet and waved her arm around, the kitten clinging gleefully to the end of it.

Mrouwl sprang to her feet and hissed. “Stop that at once!” though no-one was sure whether she was talking to the terrified girl or the increasingly dizzy kitten.

Bryony sprang to the animal’s rescue and carefully disengaging its claws she carried it away, speaking soothingly and stroking it.

Ivy’s eyes were streaming. Surprisingly she paid no attention to the blood dripping from her hand as she rummaged in her basket. “Oh dear," she snuffled, "Where's that handkerchief?" As is usual in these instances, her body was shaken by a volley of explosive sneezes just before she located the square of rather grubby fabric.

"I'b terribly thorry," she explained, dabbing at her nose and eyes. "Furry adibals ob eddy kide alwayth affect be like thith! Aaachoo!"

"Oh you poor thing!" shouted Betel with a triumphant gleam in his eyes. He trod hard on the Magician's foot. "A FUR ALLERGY can be a dreadful handicap - can't it *The*?"

"What? Er, oh yes - of course - a fur allergy? .... Oh what a shame!" Comprehension suddenly lit up the Magician's face. "I have a lot of furry creatures in my act you know. I've loved small furry creatures since I was little. Surrounded myself with them in fact. I can't feel at home without a few furry creatures around me. Would you like to meet Flopsy? He's a member of the genus Lagomorpha you know. He's very affectionate. And very furry. Now where can he have got to?" He began searching through his pockets in an absent minded sort of way.

Ivy was racked by another barrage of sneezes. "No thag you!" she gasped. "Goth, ith that the tibe? I really mutht be gettig bag! Thag you for a lubbely evedig! Cub odd Aundie Biddy." Still dabbing at her streaming eyes, she snatched up her basket and rushed out into the night.

The Magician heaved a sigh of relief. "Bryony," he said, "You must give that kitten my share of the meat tomorrow. He's earned it!"

Chapter 14

Returning to the village from a trip down to the swimming pool, the Magician and Betel saw that a crowd had gathered. "Oh sirs," sobbed old Chive. "It's my poor Bryony. My Lord Falcon's grandson tried to take her into the forest and she rejected him. Now he says that she has damaged his reputation and his honour demands that she be punished!" In the centre of the crowd a young member of the ruling class, flanked by two warriors (both built like wattle and daub outhouses) was screaming abuse at the girl. She had rejected his heavy-handed advances and *he* was insulted! Tiring of name calling he hurled her to the ground and backing off a few yards he drew his bronze knife. "A bronze axe head says I can take off her left ear with the first throw," he told his grinning companions. Betel, who still hadn't managed to put his feelings for the cooper's daughter into words, rushed to her and helped her to her feet. Standing in front of her, he faced the warriors. "That's enough of that," he said menacingly.[1]

"Get out of the way," spat the enraged nobleman. "Or it'll be your blood that my knife drinks!" He hurled his knife, only to watch Betel pluck it impossibly out of the air and then fling it up high in a glistening arc. The lordling snatched another knife from one of his warriors and threw that, following up with the knife of his other companion. Disbelief silenced the compound as all three knives spun above Betel's head in a vicious circle of glittering death. Betel smiled coldly at his young assailant. "Call yourself a knifeman, rube?" Suddenly three knives streaked across the intervening space and stuck quivering between their respective owners' feet.

For a long few seconds no-one spoke or moved. "You're good," exclaimed the warrior grudgingly. "Very good! Take the girl - she lives for just as long as she remains under your protection!" Leaving their knives still quivering in the dirt he and his escort wheeled and strode out of the compound.

---

[1]Actually, it's rather hard to say anything menacingly and be taken seriously when your most obvious attribute is a big red nose - but it was a good effort.

Slowly the crowd dispersed, leaving the two young people standing in the middle of the village with their arms locked around each other. “Oh Betel,” breathed the flushed and panting maiden. “Oh Bryony,” sighed Betel.

“Oh good grief,” muttered the Magician and he stomped off to sit in his compartment and think about poor helpless Gloria, lost and afraid somewhere on this benighted planet.

Much later, Chive found Betel and handed him the three bronze knives. “These belong to you now young Master.”

“I don’t understand,” said Betel. “Why did they go off without them like that? I thought bronze knives were highly valued around here.”

“That they are, Master, but they couldn’t pick them up, don’t you see? They tried to kill you and failed. You had it in your power to kill them. If they had accepted their weapons back from you, they would have been bound to serve you for the rest of their lives.”

“Now I get it,” said Betel with a wry smile. “It’s the law of the juggle!”

Chapter 15

The Magician looked up from the row of beans that he was hoeing and leaned on his hoe. “It always takes a disaster,” he said.

Betel paused in his assault on a particularly tough patch of squich. “Sorry?”

“I’ve got this friend,” explained the Magician. “He was a Starship Captain, very talented, bound to make Admiral one day. Of course, in his job, he was as stressed as hell. He used to talk about his pastoral dream. He said he’d give it all up, and buy a smallholding in some remote spot. Said he’d raise goats and live alongside nature, leave the rat race and learn to relax.”

“Everybody says that kind of thing.” Betel chewed on the end of a stalk of grass. “Nobody ever actually does it.”

“He contracted a weird disease of the nervous system,” explained the Magician. “They said there was no cure. They told him to give up his job. Avoid stress. They put him on a strict diet and told him that exercise was very important. That was fifteen years ago.”

“Go on.”

“A week before we joined this cruise, I was at home. I kept my parents’ house on after they both passed away. The gutters needed a coat of paint and so I’d got out the scaffolding. I was five metres off the ground with a paintbrush in one hand, clutching the bedroom window frame with the other, and both my knees shaking like maracas at Carnival time. I used to be able to run up and down ladders like a monkey. Now I’m forty-one and suddenly I’m old. Just then, a floater pulled up outside, and out jumped my friend the ex-Starship Captain.”

“Don’t tell me,” said Betel, “let me guess.”

“Right! He was fit and sun tanned. Radiating health! He ran up the ladder and bounced onto the platform alongside me as if it was the safest place in the world. He’d just got back from a walking holiday on the continent. The diet and the exercise were obviously suiting him down to the ground, and he was totally un-stressed. He was enjoying every moment of life to the full. Chronologically, he’s ten years older than I am. Physically, he's ten years younger."

"I get it," said Betel, "it took a disaster to make him change his life style."

"And it took a disaster to make me change mine!" The Magician shifted his grip on the hoe. "I've been doing a second-rate conjuring act on cruise liners and in seedy cabarets for twenty-two years. Hating myself for doing it. All that time I've promised myself that one day I'd throw it all up and settle down. Live a simple life with the woman I love. When I find poor Gloria, I'm going to build us a house here in this village, raise children, grow my own food and nothing is ever going to make me leave."

Old Chive stumbled panting into the field. "They've come," he gasped.

"Let me guess," said Betel. "You ordered a pair of thermal long johns from a mail order shopping catalogue?"

"Ignore him, Chive," said the Magician. "What have come?"

"Chive took a deep breath and spoke slowly, as if addressing a child. "It's not a what - it's a they. They're Wizard-priests and they've come to take you to the seminary. Please come quick, it don't do to keep 'em waiting!"

As they walked back to the village, Chive explained about the Wizard-priests. They were the servants of the Sky God. They were also the guardians of the magic. They lived in a religious community, spending their time in prayer and contemplation, learning the spells and rituals and in honest labour, for the community was largely self-supporting. Since the priesthood was an all male affair, novices had to come from outside. Whenever a young man in one of the villages discovered that he could work some minor magic and was in need of guidance, the Wizard-priests seemed to know. No-one knew how they knew - but they knew. "Oh yes," said old Chive. "Three years ago, when that oldest lad of Grog's started lighting the kiln of a morning without even bothering to get out of his bed, they knew. Two days later a couple of 'em walked into the village as bold as brass, and they took him. His feet never touched the ground!"

Chive noticed the looks of disbelief on the faces beside him. “Really!” he said.

The two Wizard-priests were waiting outside the door of Chive’s house. They were dressed in long grey robes, belted with rope and they were carrying staffs of curiously carved dark wood. The patterns seemed to twist and writhe if you looked at them for very long and it was noticeable that most of the curious villagers who had come to watch were pointedly not looking at the staffs. The strangers also had long beards and the kind of eyebrows that make glowering inevitable. They didn’t waste any time.

“You are the one that they call The Magician,” said the one on the left. “I am Brother Deepstone and this,” he indicated his companion, “is Brother Bloodmoon. You will come with us.” They turned and began to walk towards the wicker gate.

After a few paces they stopped and turned around. Slowly. “Now,” said Brother Bloodmoon.

The Magician still didn’t move. Ever since Biddy had tried to marry him off to the unfortunate Ivy, he’d been feeling rebellious. “You forgot to say please,” he said.

Brother Deepstone may have smiled. Under all that rather yellowish beard he could have been doing almost anything. “You have two choices,” he explained. “You can walk out of here under your own power, or you can leave without your feet touching the ground. Frankly I’d enjoy the latter, but you can make your own decision. So come on Sunshine, make my day!”

The Magician glanced at Brother Deepstone’s staff. The patterns stopped writhing and, almost as if they were embarrassed, they arranged themselves in a rigid display of total immobility. “You still forgot to say please,” he said, mildly.

Years of dealing with people whose belief in their powers went bone deep had left the two Wizard-priests totally unable to envisage a situation in which their magic might prove less than irresistible. Brother Deepstone raised his hand. He made a dramatic gesture in the direction of the Magician. There was a damp fizzing sound and a weak green spark dripped from his finger tip and fell onto the ground by his sandal. It ran around for a second or two, looking for somewhere to hide, and then it crept under a stone.

Underneath his beard, Brother Bloodmoon may have snarled. He raised his staff, sighted along its length and muttered something that sounded vaguely obscene. Nothing happened. Obviously puzzled, Bloodmoon reversed his staff and peered at its end like an absent-minded western gunfighter looking down the barrel of a recalcitrant Colt 45. The delayed blast of magic took off both his magnificent eyebrows and left little more than a fringe of beard. It smouldered gently.

"Please?" he said.

****

The afternoon was warm and it was a long walk to the seminary. Even Deepstone and Bloodmoon were grateful that the Magician had refused to leave the village until Bryony had prepared a picnic basket. As they all sat on a patch of grass overlooking a bubbling stream, sharing bread and crumbly white cheese, Betel tried to understand what was going on.

"So no-one is allowed to do magic unless he's got a license from you lot - is that it?"

"Lie sense?" Deepstone looked puzzled. "What does lie sense mean?"

"What I mean is, nobody's allowed to do magic without your permission, - right?"

Brother Bloodmoon shook his head. "Magic is the gift of the Sky Father," he said. "Only He decides who is worthy. We simply undertake to train and prepare those He has chosen."

The Magician plucked a small yellow flower from the grass and twirled its stem between his fingers. "What if the chosen one doesn't want to be trained?" he asked.

Bloodmoon picked absently at a patch of charred hair on his cheek. "We show him the error in his thinking," he said. He looked up to see Betel favouring him with a cynical grin.

"No magic without a license," Betel repeated.

"Come on then," said the Magician, scrambling to his feet, "let's go and see if they're going to grant me a license."

Two hours later, the travellers got their first look at their destination. From the brow of a low hill they could see a number of huts surrounded by a ditch and bank. It was not unlike their own adopted village, except that at the centre was a building bigger than any they had seen so far on this planet.

Deepstone pointed proudly. "The seminary," he said.

Before they reached the seminary, a large number of people had turned out to meet them. All were male, most were bearded, and no small number had eyebrows as magnificent as those still sported by Brother Deepstone. All wore the long grey woollen robes and rope belt, and all carried the carved wooden staff and bronze knife.

As they all marched through the entrance of the compound and up to the enormous timber building, the Magician felt like a prisoner with a military escort.

The building itself was made of six concentric circles of vertical wooden posts. The posts in the third circle were thicker and taller than the others. The roof sloped up from the eaves on the outermost circle, reached the high ridge on the third circle and then sloped down again to the inner eaves, leaving an unroofed area in the centre which admitted light and air. The general gloom inside the building made the unroofed central area seem even brighter. Standing in the circle of sunlight was a snowy-haired Wizard-priest wearing a robe of purest white. He shone like an angel.

"Kneel before the Archmage," hissed Bloodmoon.

"I don't think so," replied the Magician, a little surprised at himself. He'd never been so assertive before. "Perhaps," he thought, "it's something to do with this planet?"

Bloodmoon and Deepstone stepped smartly aside. The Archmage

swung up his staff and muttered something under his breath. Betel's knees folded abruptly and he crumpled to the ground.

The Archmage looked at the Magician. He seemed surprised. Again he aimed his staff but this time his voice rang around the building. "BLAST YOU!"

Nothing happened.

The Archmage looked puzzled. He began to reverse his staff with the obvious intention of examining the business end.

"Noooooo!" Brother Deepstone hurled himself across the intervening space. His shoulder charge knocked his ancient mentor aside as he snatched the staff from the old one's grip. There was a loud thunderclap and a brilliant discharge of bluish light.

The Magician's eyes were watering. He rubbed at them with the back of his hand.

The Archmage staggered to his feet. His sight was totally obscured by yellow blobs and streaks. "Deepstone," he bellowed, "just what the hell do you think you're ..... "

Into his clearing vision swam the unfocussed face of his second in command. His robe was charred and blackened and his features were sooty. Of his beard and eyebrows there remained not a trace. The little that remained of his hair was smoking. "Did it ... save you," apologised the char-grilled Wizard, swaying uncertainly. "Knew .... was going ... backfire!" He fell over backwards.

Betel examined the carbonized features of the peacefully recumbent Deepstone. He allowed his gaze to take in the almost hairless face of Bloodmoon and then he looked into the eyes of their leader. "Looks like you've got a matched pair," he commented. "Want to go for a full set?"

The Archmage ground his teeth. His face reddened until it rivalled the by now setting sun. He trembled like a previously quiescent volcano about to forgo the habit of centuries. Throughout the enormous building, Wizard priests began backing away, shaking their heads prayerfully, their hands held palm outwards in front of them.

Brother Bloodmoon took a step towards him. "Sire," he ventured, "I wouldn't recommend .... "

The spiritual leader of the most powerful convocation of Wizard priests in the Northern Hemisphere took a deep breath. He let it out slowly. "All right," he gritted, "you are the only man I have ever met whose disbelief is rigid enough to protect him from my magic. But there is still no-one in this world who has the power to work magic <u>against</u> me. I am the most potent channel of the Great God's force alive!"

He drew himself up to his full height and pointed at the Magician with an outstretched finger.

"I challenge you!" His voice boomed and echoed through the great hall. "Work even one trivial spell against me and I will own that you are my successor, the new and rightful heir to my seat and to the loyalty of all these," his gesture encompassed all of the massed Wizards, "the Sky Father's priesthood!"

The Magician smiled. "All I wanted was a license," he murmured.

He turned slowly through a full circle, his hands held out in front of him, their fingers splayed, demonstrating that he was holding nothing. Then he reached out his hand towards his opponent. The old Wizard's face creased with the effort of projecting maximum disbelief. He was good at it. From behind the Archmage's ear, the Magician withdrew ONE red billiard ball.

One was enough. In a world where everyone understood the reality of magic, trickery had never been envisaged. As one man, the puissant priests of the mighty Sky God fell to their knees.

Chapter 16

Moments before, the noise of conversation had filled the refectory. It was silent now as Brothers Deepstone and Bloodmoon showed the Magician and Betel to their places at the top table. Everyone stood expectantly. "What now?" whispered the Magician out of the corner of his mouth.

"Beats me," replied Betel, "but they all seem to be waiting for something!"

Brother Bloodmoon leaned across from their left. "They're waiting for YOU," he hissed, "no-one can sit down until you do."

The two friends sat down and with an audible sigh, the rest of the brotherhood assumed their seats. Novices scurried between the tables bringing freshly baked bread and bowls of soup.

The Magician shifted uncomfortably. The white robe he was wearing had belonged to the previous incumbent and it was far too small. Betel, as the new Archmage's right hand man, had been given the grey robe of an adept. It was several sizes too large and he was busily rolling up the sleeves so that they wouldn't trail in the soup.

"Pssst!" Brother Bloodmoon was trying to attract their attention again. He nodded apologetically towards the other diners. "No-one can start their meal until you do - Master," he explained.

The Magician picked up the bread and tore off a lump. Instantly the room was filled with the sound of clattering spoons and the slurping of soup. He lifted a spoonful of soup to his lips. It was made from a variety of root vegetable and was rather bland.

"What's the meat course tonight?" he asked brother Deepstone.

"Meat?" If the Wizard-priest had possessed eyebrows they would have disappeared into his hairline[1]. "We don't eat meat! It weakens the body and interferes with our ability to perform magic."

---

[1]If he'd possessed a hairline for them to disappear into.

Betel didn't look surprised. "I'll bet you don't touch alcoholic drink either, do you?" He nudged his friend with an urgent elbow. "We've got to get out of here. Give the old chap his job back and let's go home."

"You don't understand." Deepstone was shaking his head. "Abdication isn't allowed. There's only one way to stop being the Archmage. Death!"

"The reluctant holder of the title looked unhappy. "But my predecessor wasn't killed," he argued, "I just pulled a ball out of his ear."

"He is meditating in his cell," explained Brother Bloodmoon, "in preparation for the sepulture ceremony tomorrow morning."

Betel choked on his soup. "I think I'd like a word with him," said the Magician thoughtfully.

Brother Deepstone beckoned to a pair of burly brothers at the nearest table. "The Archmage wants to see the prisoner," he said. "Drag him over here immediately."

"No, no, - please don't do that. Just invite him to join me for a little chat."

The two adepts marched off looking rather puzzled. They returned in almost no time, shepherding the old Wizard between them.

"Thank you for coming," said the Magician. "Please, sit down. Brother Deepstone has explained to me the rather permanent nature of this job."

The old man's eyes brightened. "Having second thoughts, were you? Heh, heh! Well, you can't! There's only one way out, the way I'll be taking tomorrow. It's the will of the Sky Father."

"Just suppose," said the reluctant Archmage, "that there was some way to discover the real will of the Sky God in this matter. Wouldn't that take precedence over tradition?"

The ex-incumbent reflected for a moment. "What you're talking about is augury," he said. "We've never had much truck with that. The entrails of a pigeon can be made to say almost anything."

The Magician smiled. "Perhaps there's a more reliable way," he said. "Betel, I wonder if you'd mind fetching a pack of cards from my jacket pocket?"

Betel looked a little apprehensive at the thought of invading the jacket again, but he hurried off. If his friend had thought of a way out of this, then Betel would do anything he could to help!

With a pack of cards in his hands, the Magician felt much more in control of the situation. "Now then," he began, fanning out the cards, "these cards are a kind of - er - almanac. There are fifty-two cards, one for every week of the year. There are four suites, one for each of the seasons. Each suite contains thirteen cards, the number of lunar months in a year." He held up the King of Hearts. "Here is the King, symbolizing the, er, Sky God, and the Queen representing the Earth Mother. The Jack is the Archmage."

He riffled the cards, fanned them out again face downward and offered them to the old Wizard-priest. "Take a card," he said, "any card."

The old man reached for a card, hesitated and took one from elsewhere in the pack. The Magician also selected a card and put down the pack on the table. He turned over his card. It was the Jack of Hearts. The two burly Wizards who had brought the deposed Archmage in, grabbed him again by the elbows.

"No! Stop!" The Magician's voice was imperious. "Look at his card first!"

Brother Deepstone turned it over. It was the Jack of Spades.

"We cannot both rule," said the deposed leader. It was a flat statement of fact.

"True. We must ask the Sky Father to show us his will."

The Magician fanned out the cards again. He inserted his card into the pack, somewhere near the middle. "Please do the same," he said, proffering the pack to his rival. He shuffled the cards thoroughly. "Betel," he said, choosing the only person present who would understand, "please cut the pack."

Betel cut the pack twice and re-assembled it. He then allowed Deepstone and Bloodmoon to do the same. He placed the pack face downwards on the table.

The Magician reached out one hand. "Who will be chosen?" he asked. He tapped the pack with his index finger, then he turned over the top card. It was the Jack of Spades. "Congratulations," he said, "the will of the Sky Father is clear."

"Ha!" With a shout of triumph, the re-appointed Archmage leapt to his feet. He took the next card from the pack. It was the Jack of Hearts. Slowly and deliberately, he tore the card into tiny fragments and scattered them across the table. "Tomorrow," he exulted, "you die in my place!"

Betel groaned.

The Magician smiled sadly. "Is that really His will?" he asked. He turned over the pack and spread them out for everyone to see. All of the cards were identical Jacks of Hearts.

The Archmage thought quickly. He knew that he had only been reprieved by the fall of one card. If he questioned this latest sign, his own position might again be in question. He made up his mind.

"The Sky Father has spoken," he announced. "You shall not die. But you cannot remain in this place. I hereby appoint you a lay brother, free to go out and live in the world beyond our gates and practise your magic for the good of all His people."

Betel whistled. "You know what?" he said. "I think he just gave you a license!"

Chapter 17

When the Magician and Betel left the village to go to the seminary, the whole village turned out to watch. Others were watching too.

In a small copse of trees slightly uphill from the village, a spoiled young nobleman and his two henchmen were crouching in the undergrowth. As the two Wizard priests and their supposed prisoners made their way down the road to the East, the young man rubbed his hands together and laughed.

"I warned that red-nosed upstart," he crowed. "She is safe as long as she remains under your protection, I said. Well, he has withdrawn his protection. Tonight she will be mine!"

Hours later the village slept at last. A gibbous moon floated in a star-filled sky and the smoky smell of fires banked up for the night lay heavy on the cool night air. In the pig sty, ponderous bodies jostled briefly for space and then subsided in grunts and sighs. From the woodland at the far edge of the fields an owl hooted, loud in the stealthy quietness of nocturnal activity.

Three shadowy figures crept into the compound. They knocked gently on the door of Chive's house. A few moments later, Chive opened the door and peered out. No-one seemed to be there. He stepped outside and peered around. "Funny!" he muttered, turning back to the doorway, "I could have sworn I heard ..... "

The two henchmen appeared suddenly. They threw a blanket over his head to smother his cries and roughly bundled the old chap off in the direction of the woodpile, where he was trussed and gagged. He was left lying very uncomfortably behind a large stack of firewood.

The young master of the two heavies slipped through the open door of Chive's house and closed it soundlessly behind him. In the flickering light of the fire he could see that the sleeping compartments nearest to the door were deserted. He crept across the large room, looking for

Bryony. Nothing could prevent him now from finishing what he had begun a few days before.

He tip-toed into her cubicle. She was lying in a tangled heap of pelts. Her chestnut hair was spread out framing her angelic face and one arm was outstretched, cradling a particularly beautiful fur - golden, soft and fluffy. Seeing her lying there, so lovely, so defenceless he felt a sudden wave of heat envelop his body. Breathing heavily he pulled off his leggings and slipped his tunic over his head.

He lifted one of the skins and slipped underneath it. She stirred in her sleep. The intruder put his hand over her mouth and as her body stiffened he whispered, "Don't make a sound or the old man gets it!"

Two amber eyes opened amongst the fluffy golden fur. Lips slid back to reveal wickedly sharp teeth, bared in a vicious snarl. A hiss like a basket full of adders confirmed that he and Bryony were not alone.

The two bodyguards were sitting with their backs against the woodpile playing knuckle bones by the light of the moon. They were speaking in hushed tones of their admiration for the young man they were sworn to protect.

"Wonder how the little twerp's gettin' on?" mused the first.

"Probably be back out 'ere in a minute to ask what to do!"

"Cor! 'Ave you taken a good look at her? I could tell him what to do all right!"

"You reckon she's a virgin?"

"Not fer much longer! Any time now, I reckon."

The peace of the night was split by a series of blood curdling screams.

"She's got a good pair of lungs on her! I wonder what he's doin' to make her scream like that?"

"That's not her you berk! That's 'im! Oh Gawd, he's woken up the village!"

Men began to tumble out of the houses. There weren't many real weapons in the village, but the collection of axes, pitchforks and other sharp tools being wielded looked pretty lethal anyway. There were two muffled thuds, the kind of thuds that might have been produced if two large men had climbed over the palisade and fallen into the ditch on the other side.

The door of Chive's house burst open and a naked young man ran screaming across the compound. Blood was welling from a score of strange wounds which criss-crossed his body. Each wound was a pattern of parallel cuts. He also appeared to have been bitten in some very uncomfortable places. The runner hurled himself over the palisade and still screaming, ran off into the night.

Chapter 18

The magician had tried to make a quick exit. To be honest it had occurred to him that the newly re-instated Archmage might still try to shorten his career as a lay brother, but the day was almost gone and the other Wizard priests had been very persistent. Eventually he and Betel had agreed to stay in the guest hut for one night.

"You know what?" Betel was piling straw onto the hurdle that was to be his bed. "I'm glad we don't have to stay here. Hard beds, tasteless food and itchy clothes don't appeal to me. I don't reckon these guys know how to have fun at all."

There was a knock on the door. The Magician looked at Betel. Betel shrugged his surprise. "Come in," he said.

Brother Deepstone stepped into the hut holding a large earthenware jug. Behind him Brother Bloodmoon struggled to close the door with an elbow while clutching four beakers.

"We, er, thought you might like a nightcap," hazarded Deepstone, proffering the jug.

"That's very civil of you," allowed Betel, accepting the offering. "What is it?"

Bloodmoon coughed. "It's er, a tonic," he said, "made from honey and flavoured with a flower that grows round here."

"Come and sit down by the fire," said the Magician. "Betel, would you like to be mother?"

Betel poured four beakers of the flower tonic and they all sat, awkwardly, holding the beakers and looking at each other.

"You don't have to wait for me any more," said the Magician, "I'm only a lay brother now."

"Oh. Yes. That's right," said Bloodmoon. He took a gulp of tonic, sighed and wiped his mouth on his sleeve. "By heck, I needed that," he said.

Betel looked suspiciously at Bloodmoon. He looked suspiciously at the flower tonic. "Well, er, cheers!" he muttered. He took a tiny sip of the fluid. A happy smile slowly spread across his face. “Hey! I thought you guys didn’t drink alcohol?”

Deepstone grinned. “I never said that. Did you ever say that, Brother Bloodmoon?”

“No, I’m pretty sure that I never said that either.”

“There you are then, neither of us ever said that!”

Silence descended again, broken only by gulps and contented sighs.

Betel refilled all the beakers and sat back. Whatever this stuff was, it was having a familiar effect. He felt relaxed and companionable.

Brother Deepstone began to sing, quietly. His voice was deep and mellow.

“Wizard went a callin’ some years ago - it’s true,

Wizard went a callin’ some years ago - it’s true,

Wizard went a callin’ some years ago

I won’t tell you how I know. It’s true, I swear, it’s true.”

“What’s that?” asked Betel.

“Oh, it’s a song the novices all sing,” answered Deepstone. “They pretend it’s about the tutor they hate the most, and they make up scurrilous adventures for him. This is a relatively harmless version.”

“He knocked on Goldy Bedstraw’s door - it’s true,

He knocked on Goldy Bedstraw’s door - it’s true,

He knocked on Goldy Bedstraw’s door

He’d never been round there before. It’s true, I swear, it’s true.”

“Another nightcap anybody?” Betel passed the jug around again. “What happened when she answered the door?”

"She asked him in to take some tea - it's true,

She asked him in to take some tea - it's true,

She asked him in to take some tea

Said, there's something you can do for me! It's true, I swear, it's true."

"I think I know how this is going to turn out," said the Magician. "These stories always end in disaster. Don't I remember somebody saying that sex weakens a Wizard's magical powers?"

"That's right," agreed Brother Bloodmoon, holding out his beaker for another refill.

"What happened next I cannot tell - it's true,

What happened next I cannot tell - it's true,

What happened next I cannot tell

But his magic powers were shot to hell! It's true, I swear, it's true."

"Thash very good," Betel observed, "but I've never had any magic sho I don't shuppose I'd mish it!"

"I wouldn't care!" The Magician stood up unsteadily and glared at the others. "If I could find my Gloria, I'd marry her like a shot, and the magic could go hang!"

"Gloria?" Bloodmoon looked puzzled. "Who's Gloria, and what do you mean, if you could find her, - don't you know where she is?"

"Gloria is the most beautiful, the most sensuous, the most devashtatingly irresistible woman in the whole world!" The Magician took another swig of the tonic. "She's somewhere lost and alone on thish planet, and if I knew where she was, I'd go and rescue her like a shot!" He sat down suddenly.

"Have you tried scrying?" asked Bloodmoon.

"Sh..crying? What's shcrying?"

Deepstone grinned. “How can any magician as powerful as you not know how to scry?” he asked. “Come on, we’ll show you.”

The Magician shook his head sadly. “It’sh kind of you,” he said, “but you shee, I don’t think I believe in magic.”

“Brother Bloodmoon and I believe in magic. All we have to do is lower your resistance a little and together we might be able to do it. - Have another drink.”

It was touch and go which would weaken first, the Magician’s resistance to belief in magic, or the ability of his knees to support him. He stood unsteadily between the two Wizard priests, gripping both their staffs and staring at a large polished bronze mirror which Betel was holding in front of him with both hands. Despite himself he could feel the magical power of the two adepts coursing through the staffs and into his body.

The mirror clouded, then it began to clear. He was looking down on something golden and shiny. It was hair, long, silky blonde hair. With this realization the image cleared more quickly. He was looking at his dear Gloria lying fast asleep on a woollen blanket. There was something clutched in her hand. It looked like, yes, it was a crumpled white flower. He reached out to touch her and his fingers brushed the bronze mirror. Gloria began to grow smaller and smaller. He realised that his viewpoint was getting higher and higher.

He passed through the roof of Gloria’s house and kept rising, high into the air. Soon he could see the village spread out beneath him. Higher and higher he rose until the whole country seemed to be spread out like a map, and then he began to fall. The world rushed up at him but now he was centred on the wizards’ seminary. He passed harmlessly through the roof of the guest hut and back into his own body.

His two new friends walked the sagging body of the sleeping Magician to his pallet and drew a blanket over him. He was smiling.

Bloodmoon whispered to Betel, “I’m sure it worked. Don’t go tomorrow without saying goodbye, and if there’s ever anything else we can do to help ... ”

Betel nodded and smiled gratefully. “Goodnight.”

The next morning they slept rather late. Breakfast turned out to be a bowl of porridge, salty and made with water. There was no sign of the Archmage but the brothers that they met greeted them cordially enough.

"If you were a real magician," groaned Betel, "you'd be able to cure my aching head."

"If I were a real magician," replied his bleary-eyed companion, "I'd be able to cure MY aching head!"

They were just about ready to leave when Bloodmoon and Deepstone came to say goodbye.

"Where are you heading for?" asked Deepstone.

"Don't mention the word *head*," muttered Betel.

"Oh dear, a man who can't hold his booze."

"That wasn't booze! I've temporarily contained every kind of booze in the universe, and that rotgut definitely wasn't any of them. That was Fomalhautean Viper[1] venom!"

"What you need is a hair of the dog that bit you." Brother Deepstone proffered a familiar jug.

"Oh no! When I want to be hospitalized I'll do something relatively painless - like chewing off my own leg!"

"In that case," Bloodmoon grinned, "take it with you as a leaving present. Perhaps one day you'll want to celebrate something with a real man's drink."

"Thank you," said the Magician. "In answer to your earlier question, we're going back to the village to make sure that everyone is all right and then we're going to look for the place where I saw Gloria."

---

[1]Fomalhautean Viper: A bad tempered serpent whose bite delivers 10 cc's of hot caustic venom into the doomed victim. (You'd be bad tempered too if you had to spend your life with a mouth full of hot caustic venom!)

“Good luck,” said Bloodmoon. “We brought something for you too. If you’re going to be doing a lot of travelling, you’ll need this.” He held out a Wizard Priest’s staff, beautifully carved and inlaid, and shod with bronze. “You’re a member of our order now and this is your badge of office. No-one will argue with you if you’re carrying it.”

“Thank you,” said the Magician. “I’ll try not to dishonour it! Goodbye!”

Chapter 19

Gloria was woken by what sounded like a riot outside the hut that she now shared with Meg. Men's voices were raised in anger and protest, women were crying and children were screaming. She tumbled out of her bed and pulled on a smock and a shawl. Despite her haste, Meg was up before her. "What's going on," Gloria demanded, "is it an invasion?"

Meg grimaced. "It must be time for the temple detail again," she said.

"Temple? What temple?"

Meg pointed. "About four, maybe five miles in that direction," she explained, "they're building a temple. They've been building it for the last fifteen hundred years, on and off. According to the Wizard-priests, the Sky God goes there every mid-summer solstice to mate with the Earth Mother, or something of the sort."

They opened the door and looked out. A grim-faced group of warriors were herding all the men and older boys of the village into a line by the gate. In the line, a distraught girl of three or four held on grimly to her daddy's sleeve while an equally tearful mother tried to persuade her to let go. One of the soldiers grunted angrily and stepped towards them. Gloria materialized right in front of him. "You don't want to involve yourself in that," she smiled. "We'll sort it out for you." The soldier felt his anger melt away as that wonderful smile irradiated him. "Right you are," he said.

The line was beginning to move out of the compound as Meg crouched down beside the little girl. "Now then, Rosie," she said, "give me your hand." Rosie looked into her eyes. She stopped crying and snuffled once or twice. Meekly she put her hand into Meg's and allowed herself to be led away. "Daddy will be back in a few days," Meg told her, "and the first thing he's going to want is a great big hug from his brave little girl! Now wave goodbye, and then you must look after your Mummy."

Gloria shook her head and sighed. "I don't believe it," she said.

"Oh, it's easy," Meg relied, "when you've taught as many girls as I have, separating them from their parents becomes a matter of course."

"That's not what I meant. I just can't believe that I'm probably doomed to spend the rest of my days on a world that accepts slavery so calmly."

"Slavery?" It was Meg's turn to be shocked. "Who said anything about slavery?"

"A squad of warriors raid the village before daybreak and march off all the men and boys to an enforced labour camp, under armed guard. What does that sound like to you?"

"It's just the way our system works. We grow crops and make goods like tools, baskets and clothes. The merchant aristocrats provide us with a ready market for our surplus and arrange the import of raw materials. They get rich from the trade and that enables them to employ warriors who protect us against raids from outside the area. They also give their patronage to the Priests of the Sky God and as part of that deal we give our labour once a year to the building of the temple. The temple pleases the Sky God and he gives us good weather and abundant crops. All the parts of our society are interdependent."

"But I thought you didn't believe in the Sky God?"

"Bless you Gloria, wherever did you get that idea? Of course I believe in the Sky God, and the Wizard priests all believe in the Earth Mother too. It's just a matter of priorities. I think that She is the most important and deserving of our worship, and they think the opposite."

"So you go to worship at the temple too?"

Meg took a deep breath and let it out slowly. "You really don't belong on this world, do you? Listen, no woman has ever stood inside the temple. It is holy to the Sky God and in the eyes of the Wizard-priests, for a woman to go there would be an act of sacrilege. We're not allowed!"

There was a spark of light burning defiantly in Gloria's eye. "Not allowed?" she repeated. "Not allowed? We'll see about that!"

"The first time I met you," said Meg thoughtfully, "I knew that you were trouble. On the other hand, right now I think you've got more to worry about than annoying the priesthood. What we need now is a good place to hide."

Gloria frowned. "Hide? Hide from what?"

"When the men from Stoneford realize that all our blokes have been taken off as temple labourers, they'll be over here to have a bit of fun! - Here, where are you going?"

"I'm going to get a knife from the hut, and then I'm going to sharpen it! Any man who thinks that I'm a poor defenceless little woman left lying around for his personal enjoyment will be going home singing soprano!"

Twenty minutes later, all the women were gathered together in the centre of the village. "This is a waste of time," said a large dark-haired woman with a child on each hip. "We should be using the time to hide all the valuables and make ourselves scarce."

"Oh yes?" Gloria wasn't convinced. "And what happens when they come? A grand game of hide and seek, with you as the prize for the men who find you all alone and helpless in your little hidey-hole? Well you can stick that for a game of soldiers! There's safety in numbers and we're better off if we stay together."

The meeting turned into a knife sharpening party.

"Not like that!" Gloria was apparently doing it all wrong. "Long strokes of the stone dearie, along the blade. You'll never get it sharp scrubbing at it like that!"

Gloria took six or seven times longer than the others to sharpen her first blade and when she held it up there was a certain amount of confusion.

"What 'ave yer done ter that knife? - 'Ere Meg, come an' 'ave a gander at this 'ere knife!"

"She's ruined it, that's what she's done!"

"Back where I come from," said Gloria, proudly holding up the planet's first serrated blade, "we call this a carving knife!" She demonstrated its cutting ability on a ham that Meg fetched from their hut, and moments later every last woman was scrubbing her stone backwards and forwards across her blade as if her life depended on it.

****

The men of Stoneford hadn't hurried. They'd had a few drinks at the brewer's house, eaten a mountain of cheese sandwiches, decided that there was plenty of time and had a few more drinks. Several earthenware jars of pickled eggs had been consumed. There'd been a lot of boasting about personal prowess, and the telling of stories that definitely wouldn't have been given airtime on any broadcasting service with even the most rudimentary form of censorship. During that there'd been a few more drinks. There'd been a belching contest .... and a few more drinks. Finally, they'd decided that it was time to go. They'd had one more for the road. Some of them had actually managed to stand up. No-one had made it as far as the door.

The brewer's wife had looked in about tea-time. She'd noted the recumbent bodies draped artlessly amidst the empties. She'd sniffed at the richly scented air in the roundhouse and then she'd taken herself off to stay with her sister's family for a few days.

****

"They're coming!" It was late morning and the two ten year-old girls had been sitting high up in a tree on look-out duty for an hour. It was almost time to hand over to the next team. "THEY'RE COMING!" They scrambled down through the dense branches and raced back towards the village.

"About flippin' time!" opined Granny Boletus. "They're gettin' sloppy! When their village drew temple duty last October, our men were over there inside of an hour an' a 'alf! I 'ate waitin' about!"

"Er, right," said Gloria, "is everybody ready? Let's give them a welcome they'll never forget!"

The raiding party that shuffled up the track to the village gates looked a little the worse for wear. Some of the men were limping and this was almost certainly because of the short sections of pointed stick which had been partially buried at random intervals along the path the previous afternoon. A couple of the raiders had scratches and bruising on their faces, possibly caused by branches along the path that had been tied back and connected to trip-lines. Most of the damage however, was undoubtedly self-inflicted.

Their leader paused just outside the gate. He rubbed his bristly cheek with one hand and licked his lips nervously. Anyone near enough to see it would have remarked that his tongue was a peculiar colour. He blinked and tried to focus blood-shot eyes. Standing in the open space between the houses were all the women of the village. At their head was a spectacularly beautiful woman with long blonde hair. She was smiling. One look at that smile made his previous state of near-terminal intoxication look like the peak of mental fitness. He hardly noticed the carpet of reeds that had been laid just inside the gate. His sluggish brain, labouring under the impact of that devastating smile, suggested that it might be a welcome mat. "Alright!" He stepped forward, flanked by two lieutenants. Their cry of alarm as the reeds gave way was instantly muffled as they fell through the opening thus revealed and into a large pit filled with a noisome mixture of water and pig excrement.

As the three men climbed out of the hole, it was clear that the experience had had one marked effect upon them. They were, for the first time in twenty-four hours, wide awake and stone-cold sober. The rest of the raiding party gingerly worked their way around the booby trap and formed up in a group behind their leader. Well behind him.

"Right!" he said in the most authoritative tones he could muster. "What's the meaning of this?"

"Gawd," commented one of the women, "doesn't he smell shocking?"

"Yeah! And even that pig shit doesn't cover it up!"

"Come on," explained the smelly one, reasonably. "You know how this works. You all go off to your huts and hide, then we come and find you. There's no need to be impatient. Everybody will get a turn." He looked at Granny Boletus, ninety if she was a day and wrinkled like one of last autumn's crab apples. She grinned coquettishly at him, exposing her only remaining tooth, a blackened stump in a sea of pink gum. "Well, - almost everyone!"

"No," said Gloria. "We're not going anywhere to be bullied one at a time by you and your hung-over cronies. We're all staying here, together, and we'll fight to the last man!"

The smeary leader of the raiding party was thrust aside by a huge man with muscular bare arms. Over his woollen shirt and leggings he wore a leather apron. Gloria guessed that he was the village bronze smith. He was grinning.

"Don't you mean you'll fight to the last woman?"

"I mean exactly what I said!" A wickedly serrated knife appeared in Gloria's hand. "This is a new invention. It's called a carving knife - and guess which bits of you we're going to carve if you come near us?"

There was a sharp intake of breath amongst the raiders. One or two of the more imaginative ones had tears in their eyes.

Gloria stepped forward. Behind her she heard the whole of her makeshift army follow. The men looked wildly around. Several of them broke out in sweat. A little ferrety fellow at the back began to sneak away furtively.

"Oh bugger this for a lark," opined the owner of the big biceps, "anybody fancy a drink?"

"Good idea," agreed the ex-leader, "I think it must be my round."

"Did you hear that? asked a portly chap with floury clothes. "I've never heard him say that before!"

"Quick then, let's take him up on it before he changes his mind!"

"Er, if you'll excuse us ladies?"

The stealthy withdrawal turned into a stampede.

"Come again any time boys," yelled Granny Boletus. Her piercing cackle chased them down the track.

Chapter 20

The Magician and Betel were looking forward to getting back to the village. They were tired, hungry and still slightly hung-over. They certainly were not prepared for the news that Mrouwl brought them. "It's Lord Falcon's men," she explained. "They've taken everyone in the village hostage and they say that they'll start killing people if you don't give yourselves up."

"What about Bryony?" demanded Betel.

"They've got her too," admitted the cat, "I'm sorry, there were rather a lot of them."

"If they've hurt Bryony ....." Betel began.

"They haven't yet," she told him, "but we shouldn't keep them waiting too long."

The villagers were gathered together in the middle of the enclosure. Grouped around them were a score of the meanest looking men at arms that the Magician had ever seen. Not that he'd seen many.

A giant of a man dressed mostly in stained leather and dented bronze swaggered towards them. "You've upset my Lord Falcon," he accused. "That was very stupid of you."

The Magician sighed. "What's all this about?" he asked.

"Stand aside, pretty boy," spat the leather fetishist, "it's your friend I'm talking to." He turned to Betel. "My Lord Falcon wants to see you," he grinned.

"Fine," said Betel. "I wouldn't mind a word or two with him either. Why don't you go back and tell him that I'll be round to visit just as soon as I've had a good meal and a few winks of sleep?"

"A funny man eh? Let me explain something to you, red-nose." He gestured and two of his men stepped forward. Bryony stood between them, her arms gripped firmly by their gloved hands. "My Lord Falcon said I was to take you and the girl to him, but he didn't say in how many pieces."

Betel snarled and started towards him, but the Magician pulled him back. “Well now,” he murmured, “It seems that you leave us very little choice!” He shifted his staff to the other hand, in order to get a better grip on Betel’s sleeve. The warrior’s face changed as he recognised the staff for the first time.

“Your pardon sir,” he said, pulling off his leather helmet and shuffling backwards a pace. “I didn’t realize that your honour was a Wizard-priest!”

“And that makes a difference does it?”

“Oh, yes your worship. I would never have spoken to you like that if I’d seen your staff earlier!” He eyed the staff nervously, and swallowed.

“So what you’re saying,” queried the Magician, “correct me if I’m wrong, is that it’s all right for you to bully and threaten people if they’re <u>not</u> Wizard-priests?”

The bully’s face cleared and a relieved smile brightened his craggy face. “Yes sir, that’s exactly it!” he beamed.

“You can let me go now,” said Betel coldly, “I wouldn’t dirty my hands on this reptile!”

The Magician looked at the two warriors holding Bryony. “Let her go,” he said. He turned back to their leader. “My friend and I are going to Chive’s house. We are going to get cleaned up, enjoy a hot meal and get some rest. Tomorrow we’ll go and see your employer. Now I’m going to start counting. By the time I get to ten I want you and your men outside the palisade. One, two...”

“Begging your pardon your holiness.”

“Three, four ... what is it?”

“Er, I have orders to take you back .... I mean, we have to accompany you.”

“Fine! You can wait outside the palisade until morning! Now where was I? Oh yes, five, six ....”

There was a momentary pause while all of the armed men looked at each other, and then a mad scramble for the gate.

Bryony was locked in Betel's arms and the Magician felt that he wasn't going to get much information from her for some considerable time. He went in search of Chive. "What in heaven is all this about?" he demanded.

Chive explained about the nocturnal visit that Lord Falcon's grandson had paid, and the humiliation that he had suffered a second time. "What are you going to do sir?" he asked, and the Magician was forced to admit that he had no ideas at all. "Don't worry about it though," he told Chive, "Betel and I will think of something .... I hope!"

****

Lord Falcon was puzzled. He had sent out his men the day before to round up a couple of strangers and a girl. They had not returned until late on the second day, when he had been considering sending out a second force. Then they had trooped back to the stockade. Worse, instead of dragging in the prisoners, or prodding them at sword point, they had marched in ahead of them, obviously under the orders of the tall one with the staff.

The residence was built on high ground. Although superficially similar to the other buildings that the friends had seen on this planet, it was bigger, grander and more imposing than any, except the great hall at the seminary. There were few animals in evidence and none of the men in the compound looked like farmers. There was one other difference and a rather chilling one. The high wooden walls of the stockade, and the stout wooden gates, would make it very hard for an enemy to get in .... or out!

The Magician formed up the escort outside the large roundhouse and told them to stand easy.

He rapped on the door with the heel of his staff and called out. "Anyone home?"

Inside the building a voice could be heard, muttering and grumbling. "Just a minute," it called, "dammit, where did I put my slippers? Ah!

Thank you my dear."

The door opened, affording a brief glance of highly polished carved wood and finely woven woollen hangings on the walls before the stooped frame of an old man filled the opening.

"You wanted to see us?" Betel enquired.

"I did. Please excuse the manner of the invitation, I was afraid that you might refuse." As the venerable Lord stepped out into the sunshine, two retainers hurried up with a carved and upholstered chair, the only one that the castaways had seen on this world.

"Ah!" Lord Falcon sank back into the chair with obvious relief and looked at the strangers standing in front of him. "Which one of you is the one they call Betel?" He asked.

"I am."

"My men tell me that you are a highly skilled warrior."

"They are too generous with their praise."

"Not usually!" The old man paused for a moment. "My grandson has seen sixteen summers. He is old enough to be called a man. He has chosen his warrior name. The arrogant child wishes to improve on my title. He wants to be called Eagle. " He paused as if chewing on this affront. "But first there is the rite of passage. You know what a rite of passage is?"

"It's a document that gets you past border controls isn't it?"

The Magician laughed. "No," he said, "that's a passport. He said rite not right."

"Oh!" Betel nodded. "You mean like that not very bright young teenager on Sirtis 4 who had to sleep with a woman and fight a bear before he could be called a man?"

The Magician grinned. "Yes, that's right," he said, "whatever happened to him?"

"Well," Betel was enjoying himself. "He came home three days later - filthy, his clothes in rags, covered in scratches and bruises and said, 'right, now where's this woman I've got to fight?'"

“Enough!” Lord Falcon wasn’t laughing. “My grandson has only one task to complete. He must defeat an older warrior in combat. You are that warrior!”

“I don’t understand!” Betel was out of his depth. “This place must be crawling with real warriors. Why pick on me?”

“Because tradition says that if there is a grudge between the young man and any warrior, then that is the man who must fight with him. I think that there is plenty of bad feeling between you.”

“I suppose so,” mused Betel, “but he’s come off worst twice now. If he was to apologise and promise to behave in future I’d be prepared to ...”

“No! He has come crawling back to my house twice now, defeated and disgraced. He thought that I would punish you. He believes that his relationship to me gives him the right to ill-treat and abuse people who ordinarily look to me for protection.”

“Sir,” Betel said slowly, “with the greatest of respect .....”

“That’s it exactly,” interrupted the old man, “he has no respect! He must learn respect and you have shown that you are the man who can teach it to him.”

“Hey Granddad!” A familiar voice drifted across the compound. “I see you rounded up the loser for me.” He strode across to them, his protectors shambling behind him. “Glad you could make it, scarecrow! I’m looking forward to cutting off that red nose of yours - and then I’m going to take your woman!” He leaned towards Bryony. “Get ready Beautiful, the Eagle’s gonna show you how to fly!” Mrouwl bared her teeth and he stepped away quickly. There were scabs on his forearms and cheeks, mementos of their last meeting.

“Grandson!” Lord Falcon’s voice cracked like a whip. “You will do this according to tradition! Remember the words you were taught.”

The young man paused, his lips moving silently and then he turned to Betel. “Your deeds in battle have won you great respect,” he intoned, “therefore I wish to receive my name from you. I challenge you to combat, man to man, with whatever weapons you shall choose.”

Betel stood silently for a moment, and then he turned to the old man.

Lord Falcon nodded slightly.

"I accept your challenge," Betel's voice was steady and controlled. "The weapons will be .... barrels and pigs' bladders!"

"I don't understand!"

"It's easy," Betel smiled, "We inflate the pigs' bladders and use them to try to knock each other off the barrels. I hope you've got a good sense of balance."

The young man's cockiness had evaporated. He was red-faced with anger. "This is an insult!" he spat. "Grandfather, tell him he can't do this to me. He's got to fight me properly!"

Lord Falcon pursed his lips. "It is an unusual choice of weapons," he admitted. "But to win you will need balance, strength, speed and the ability to anticipate your opponent's moves - it is a test worthy of a warrior." He smiled and continued. "Furthermore, in a normal contest you could lose your life. This way you can only lose your dignity - and you value that much too highly!"

He turned to Betel. "Tomorrow you shall fight," he said, "but tonight I invite you and your friends to join me in a feast."

Betel was puzzled again. "A feast before the contest?"

"Certainly. Tomorrow one of you will be the winner and one the loser. Tonight we can toast you both, impartially."

"Then thank you," said Betel, "we accept. What's on the menu?"

Lord Falcon allowed his sense of humour to show at last. "Two pigs!" he chortled.

The cold early-morning light seeped stealthily under the door of the guest house, only to find Betel and the Magician wide awake and discussing the morning's business.

"Cheer up Betel, you could beat the young idiot with one hand behind your back."

“That’s just the problem. He already hates me. If I go out there this morning and knock him off his barrel, he’ll spend the rest of his life looking for ways to kill me!”

“So let him win.”

“But you heard him .... he’s already told everyone that he bases his claim to Bryony on the fact that he’s going to beat me in this duel!”

“Perhaps you should have chosen a more lethal sort of combat after all.”

“Come on *The*! You know me better than that! I’ll happily knock him off a barrel, but I’m not sure that I could kill him .... even in self-defence!”

There was a knock on the door and a voice called out, “Time for breakfast, gentlemen. The contest begins when the sun is over the trees.”

Breakfast turned out to be a selection of cold meats left over from the banquet. They looked less appetizing in the cold grey light filtering through the mist that still clung to the hillside. Two pigs’ bladders had been cleaned and inflated. They sat at one end of the table like left-over balloons amidst the debris of the previous night’s revels.

“So you didn’t run away during the night then? It seems that I’ve lost a wager!” The hearty voice belonged to Lord Falcon’s grandson. He was carving lumps of pork from a large cold joint and stuffing them into his mouth as though he was half starved. “Have some of this meat .... you may be ashamed to eat in the company of warriors after I’ve thrashed you!”

“No thanks,” said Betel. “I don’t feel like eating right now.”

“What’s the matter?” enquired the lordling. “Don’t you like pig?”

“Oh, it’s not that. I just don’t want to eat with one.”

The young man’s face darkened and the knuckles of the hand gripping his knife whitened. “Why, you red-nosed peasant! How dare you talk to me like that?”

“Peasant?” Lord Falcon’s quiet voice could be heard clearly all over the compound. “You told me yourself that this man was a warrior. If he is only a peasant, how can he give you your name?”

“He insulted me! He called me a pig, and everybody knows that it’s against the rules to bait your opponent before a combat!”

Lord Falcon’s voice grew even quieter and somehow more dangerous. “Everyone knows? You know, certainly. I have given you the best teachers. But it was you who began the business of hurling insults, in spite of all that you know. Let us hope that you are more skilled with a pig’s bladder than you are with words or you will lose to this man twice today.” He gestured with one hand and the large warrior who had escorted the friends to this place stepped forward to act as Master of Ceremonies.

The MC cleared his throat and waited for silence. “My Lords, Ladies and Gentlemen! We are gathered here this morning to witness a bout between the red-nosed warrior Betel in the blue corner, and in the red corner, the grandson of My Lord Falcon, who should he emerge victorious, will henceforth be known as Lord Eagle. The contestants will fight with (ahem) pigs’ bladders whilst balanced on the two (ggrahaha) barrels now being carried into the ring. (Hmnph) One fall, one submission or (ahagrahaha) one knockout to decide the winner!” He stalked out of the ring, choking on barely suppressed laughter.

The referee called the two contestants into the centre of the ring. He placed a hand on each man’s shoulder and bent forward until their three heads were almost touching. His shoulders were also shaking. “Now then lads,” he said, “I want to see a good clean fight. No, er, er ... well, none of that anyway! Now go back to yer corners and come out er, er, (hahahaha) on barrels!”

The young man had obviously spent much of the night practising. As soon as the bell rang he pedalled his barrel across to the blue corner at high speed, swinging his bladder in a horizontal arc. Betel ducked under the blow and spun his barrel almost onto its end as he circled and headed for the relatively empty centre of the ring.

“Come on Betel!” shouted the Magician, “give him what for!”

The young warrior drove straight at Betel again and again Betel ducked under his blow, but this time he straightened up and as his opponent rolled past he swung his bladder at the youth’s head.

With a gasp of surprise the would-be warrior spun to face his enemy .... just in time to receive another blow, this time to the face. He began to step back, remembered just in time where he was and windmilled his arms in an effort to regain his balance. He straightened up, panting, and looked for his persecutor. A heavy blow across the right ear made him turn, but the next blow was from the left. "Stand still and fight like a man," he gasped and found himself unexpectedly face to face with Betel. As he drew back his arm Betel's bladder hit him again and his barrel began to move forward as his body fell inexorably backwards.

One moment the crowd was cheering wildly and the next you could have heard a pin drop. As the young nobleman's barrel spun out of the ring his body hovered a few inches above the ring. With a sweep of his arm he knocked Betel's legs from under him and Betel tumbled to the ground.

"That's not fair," Bryony shouted, "he's using magic!"

"I win!" yelled Lord Eagle. "He touched the ground first!" Suddenly he was aware of two pairs of sandaled feet. He looked up, taking in the belted robes, the carved wooden staffs and the white stubbly chins.

"You are the one they call Lord Eagle," said the one on the left. "I am brother Deepstone and this," he indicated his companion, "is brother Bloodmoon. You will come with us. Now!" The two Wizard-priests walked towards the gate, the newly qualified Lord Eagle bobbing along behind them like a toy boat on a piece of string. "Hello *The*," they said in unison as they passed, and then they and the young Lord were gone.

The MC rubbed his eyes. "His feet never touched the ground!" he gasped.

"Well!" said Lord Falcon, reaching for a beaker of wine, "My grandson is going to be a Wizard-priest. I didn't think he had it in him. This calls for a drink!"

The Magician looked thoughtful. "It means he'll never be able to inherit your mantle," he mused.

"Damn right!" The old man grinned. "Drinks all round!"

Chapter 21

Although Lord Falcon had promised that she was now under his personal protection, Betel declared that he wasn't going to leave Bryony alone again. The Magician agreed, saying that he wasn't going to be away for long and in any case he now had the protection of the Wizard's staff.

It was a sad little group of people who stood on the hillside below the village a few days later and watched the figure of their friend as he slowly dwindled in the distance.

The Magician had never been alone since arriving on this planet, and was determined to enjoy this unaccustomed privacy. He whistled several of his favourite tunes, sang a song or two and even recited a poem. Twenty minutes later he had to admit to himself that he really missed Betel's company.

"What's that?" He'd been hearing a rustling noise in the bushes near the path for some time without really stopping to wonder what it was, but suddenly some of the less welcome possibilities began to suggest themselves to him. He gripped his staff more tightly. "Come on out, - I know you're in there."

The bushes rustled a little more and then out stepped - the cat.

"Princess, I'm so glad to see you! I thought it was, - that it might be, - oh you know!"

"No," growled the cat, "I don't think I do. Who were you expecting? Not me certainly, - I wasn't invited."

"Oh! Look, I'm sorry if I offended you. It never occurred to me that you'd want to come along. I thought you were friends with Bryony."

"We are friends, but she doesn't understand anything I say. It's difficult to hold an intelligent conversation when it's so one-sided. Besides, now that Betel's back he's become very protective and I think I'm only going to be in the way."

"Then please, come along with me." The Magician thought fast. "I'd be glad of the company and I'll bet you're much better than I am at finding your way around. I'd probably get hopelessly lost without you."

The cat sat down and began to wash a paw. "Thank you," she purred, "I'd love to come along and look after you."

There was another disturbance amongst the bushes. It seemed to be heading their way. The Princess looked up at the sky and sighed. "Oh no," she breathed. "Please God, no!"

A ball of stripy fur with a bushy tail and whiskers burst out of the undergrowth. As it landed on the path it tripped over one of its big paws and rolled right over before it bumped into Mrouwl and fell on its back with its feet in the air. "Hungry," it shouted, "HUNGRY!"

"Hello little feller," said the Magician, scratching it behind the ears, "are you looking for your Mum?"

"I," said Mrouwl with all the hauteur she could summon, "am most assuredly NOT its mother."

"Well, it thinks you are."

"Just look at it," said the Princess in tones of utter despair. "It has all the grace and dignity of a pair of Doc Martins, coupled with the mental agility of an automatic washing machine, and you dare to suggest that we're related?"

"Oh come on, Princess, the kid's just hungry."

"Oh yes," agreed the cat, "it's hungry all right - it's always hungry!"

"HUNGRY!" agreed the kitten enthusiastically.

The Magician rummaged in his bag. "What would you say to a nice ham sandwich?" he asked.

"HUNGRY!"

"'Hello nice ham sandwich,' would have been a wittier rejoinder," muttered the cat.

"In any case," she told the Magician, "you'll never get it to eat sandwiches. This is a primitive creature of the wild, equipped by countless eons of evolution to survive on a diet of rodents, birds and insects. It won't even recognise a sandwich as edible. I suppose I'd better go and catch it a ..... well, would you look at that!"

The kitten wolfed down the sandwich, bread and all. It checked that there was no more forthcoming, licked its lips, gave its face a desultory wipe with a moistened paw and went to sleep with its chin resting on the Magician's foot.

Princess Mrouwl stared in amazement as the Magician picked up the sleeping bundle of fur and gently put it into his bag. "Whatever are you doing?" she asked.

"Well," he said, "I don't want to stay here all day, and I don't think it feels like walking."

"You're not thinking of taking it with us?"

"Somebody's got to look after the poor little thing. You said yourself it needs a diet of birds, rodents and things. You're the best hunter around, Mrouwl. It needs you."

"Something tells me I'm going to regret accepting your invitation. Come on then, where are we going first?"

"Don't laugh," said the Magician, "but all I've got to go on is a vision of Gloria that I had at the Wizards' seminary. I was very tired, dead drunk and there was magic involved. It doesn't seem like very reliable evidence, does it?"

The cat didn't laugh. "Go on," she murmured.

"After I saw Gloria, it was as if I hovered high above the land and looked down on it. If it wasn't just a drunken dream, then her village is west, maybe southwest from here."

"How far?" Mrouwl asked.

"Hard to say." He closed his eyes and tried to concentrate on the memory. "I guess if you drew a line from here, through the seminary, it would be as far again on the other side."

"Come on then," said the cat, "if we have that sort of distance to cover, let's get moving."

It was a fine day and at first they made good time. The Magician stepped out, vigorously swinging his arms and whistling an old marching song. The back of his shirt soon began to feel a little clammy but he didn't care, he was enjoying the exercise and the heady feeling that, at last, he was taking charge of his life.

They covered the first three miles in about an hour and a half. The path was quite well defined and the ground was firm. A short detour to avoid a flock of sheep which panicked at the sight of the Princess didn't cost much time and the day was passing very pleasantly.

Then the kitten decided that it wanted to get down and walk. Suddenly, their progress slowed to a crawl. Forty frustrating minutes trying to persuade it to come back down a tree didn't help anyone's mood. The cat climbed the tree. The kitten climbed higher. Soon the Princess was as high as she could go and the kitten was perched at the very end of a whippy twig forty feet above the ground and swaying alarmingly from side to side.

"For crying out loud," shouted the Magician. "Come down and leave it alone. If you climb any higher, one of you is going to end up falling!"

Not many people have heard a cat gnash her teeth. "Perhaps it'll land on its head," she ground out. "That shouldn't hurt it at all!"

They left the kitten where it was and walked on a little way. Moments later it was bouncing along beside them, purring and trying to catch the cat's tail. The Princess pinned it to the ground with one velvet paw and gave it a thorough licking. She glared at the Magician. "What're you grinning at?" she demanded.

"Nothing at all!" replied her friend. "Grinning? Me - grinning? I wasn't grinning!"

In the middle of the afternoon they topped a rise and saw the seminary sprawled across the opposite hillside.

The Magician didn't really want to visit the seminary again so soon. He had a feeling that the Archmage wouldn't be delighted to see him. Unfortunately, every path in the area seemed to be determined to deliver them there. After two lengthy detours and a good deal of wasted time they agreed to try finding a path through the dense woodland which clothed the countryside to the south of the wizards' stronghold.

"I don't like it," muttered the cat. They'd only travelled a mile or so under the dense canopy. It was dark, gloomy and somehow threatening.

"You don't like it! You're a cat for crying out loud! You're supposed to be at home in the natural environment. I'm the one who's lost, totally untutored in the mysteries of woodcraft and short on forest survival skills. And another thing - don't laugh - sorry, no offence intended - I can't shake off this silly paranoid feeling that we're being watched!"

Mrouwl fixed him with an unblinking stare. "You humans," she said, shaking her head. "You rely so much on technology that you've forgotten how to listen to your own instincts. We are being watched! They've been watching us ever since we entered this woodland, and right now they've got us surrounded!"

The Magician glanced around, trying hard to appear nonchalant. "Where?" he demanded. "Who's got us surrounded? I can't see anybody at all!"

"Keep your head still, keep looking straight ahead, now concentrate on the fuzzy edges of what you can see. You'll never see the Shee if you stare straight at them."

"Shee? Hey! You're right! I can see them!"

Concealed, not by the trees but amongst them, were thirty or so figures. Although only half visible he judged them to be half the height of a man for the most part, dark and hairy. There was something crooked or misshapen about them, knobbly knees and elbows, the hint of limbs that bent in unfamiliar ways. The cat was right, if you looked straight at them - they simply weren't there.

"You might as well come out," called the Magician, "we can see you quite plainly." Laughter ran around the circle and a stone thudded into a tree trunk behind his head. He held his hands up, their palms outward. "We mean you no harm."

"Speak for yourself," growled the Princess. In one eye-baffling movement she turned smoothly and gracefully then spurted into the greenery like a jet of water. The surprise was complete. There was a startled squeak and the laughter stopped abruptly.

The Magician looked behind him in disbelief. Princess Mrouwl was straddling one of the creatures, pinning it to the forest floor. Her jaws were around its throat and its eyes were filled with the horror of imminent death[1].

"Dell theb," growled the cat, forcing the words past the obstruction in her mouth while her relentless teeth pricked the creature's larynx, "thad he dieth unleth we receiff thufficiently imprethive guaranteeth regardig our thafedy in dith plathe."

"I'm sorry, I didn't get all of that. Could you say it again?"

"Thay wath agaid?"

"That bit about what we want to receive."

"Garanteeth! Garanteeth!"

"Oh! Yes - right! Guarantees. I get it!"

The Magician turned and found himself at the centre of a tight circle of beings so menacing that they took his breath away. Many carried stone knives while others levelled bows, the arrows aimed unwaveringly at his chest. He saw them clearly now and smelled them too, unwashed bodies rank with sweat and blood, wood smoke - and something else. Fear! He could smell the fear emanating from them! He gripped his staff more tightly. A ripple ran around the circle, a shiver of dread. So, they recognized the staff did they? They probably thought he could blast them with fire from it like Deepstone and the others. If only they knew how harmless it really was in his hands! He'd do more damage using it as a club! The thought of these creatures fearing him as a potent wizard was so incongruous, it actually made him smile. At the sight of that tight-lipped smile the encircling wights fell back a step. Nothing had changed and yet the balance of power had subtly shifted and all present recognized the fact. Feeling a little more confident he drew himself up and glared into the eyes of the tallest (and incidentally dirtiest) of their assailants. "My friend says .... "

"We know what your friend said." The voice was high, musical. "You are unusual travellers I'm thinking."

---

[1]Barring accident and violence, elves live for ever. For them there is no afterlife, no second chance, their immortality is in this dimension and they dread death far more than we can ever imagine.

The Magician looked at the speaker. It was as tall as a seven year-old child, scrawny and yet pot-bellied. Its hair was a knotted mass, filthy and so full of twigs and leaves that it resembled nothing so much as a long-deserted bird's nest. The eyes that stared back at him from the wrinkled face were yellow with vertically slitted pupils.

The Magician smiled again. "You'd be unusual where I come from, my friend," he said.

The captive gave a terrified squeal as the cat tightened her grip fractionally.

"All right, all right!" The shee gestured with one hand, palm held downwards. All the weapons were lowered. "And now, if you please, my brother's throat?"

"My friend mentioned guarantees, I think."

"Ah yes, guarantees is it?" A cunning grin revealed a black tongue, flicking over needle pointed yellow teeth. "All right then," the creature spat on its hand and held it out, "you have my word of honour!"

The Magician was not a man given to suspicion or distrust, yet even he hesitated to grasp the proffered hand, and not just because of the yellowish spittle that spattered its palm.

Mrouwl growled a warning deep in her throat and her victim whimpered. "Athk id idth nabe," she hissed.

"Pardon?"

"Oh good grieff! Athk idth nabe - whad's id called? And bake thure id dells you the druth!"

"Ah, sure enough there's no harm in my telling you," that cunning grin flickered across the creature's mouth again, "my name is Blaese."

The Magician had spent much of his career learning to read body language. The Shee's eyes had slid away from his and he was sure it was lying. He laughed, an artificial sound in his own ears but hopefully convincing enough. "My staff tells me that you lie," he bluffed. "I will only ask once more, so think very carefully before you lie to me again."

The cat underlined his threat with another squeeze of her jaws and her hostage whimpered piteously.

"All right, all right - my name is .... " The creature looked at the other elves. They were leaning forward, silent, straining to hear. It sidled up to the Magician, cupped its hands and standing on tip-toe whispered into his ear, "my name is Aldrich."

The forest shifted. It was as though a veil was lifted and reality re-asserted itself. The magician blinked. Nothing had changed in essence and yet .... there were fewer of the creatures than he had thought. They were slighter, less menacing. Their weapons although just as sharp seemed now to be held in attitudes of defensiveness.

Aldrich smiled shyly. His teeth were not pointed (although they were still yellow) and his tongue was pink and healthy. "An illusion," he explained, brushing a stray lock of reddish hair away from his brow, "designed to make us appear stronger than we really are." He giggled. "There's some pretty frightening things in these woods!" He winked one green eye at the Magician and attempted to dig him in the ribs with an elbow.

The Magician winced. Tears sprang to his eyes and he bit his lip as he tried not to fold around the agony that had blossomed in his groin.

"Ooops, sorry! I was forgetting for a moment there how uncommon tall you are!"

"It's ... quite ... alright." He forced the words between clenched teeth and concentrated on controlling his hands which were trembling with the need to clutch himself.

"If your companion is sufficiently impressed with my guarantee," the elf's eyes twinkled, "perhaps she would release my brother. He appears to be in some difficulty."

It was true. Mrouwl's captive had ceased struggling. His eyes were closed and his breathing was shallow and jerky. She lowered his head gently to the leaf-mould and stepped back. A female hurried forward, her eyes darting between the fallen elf and the terrifying creature which stood beside him. She knelt beside the limp figure and began to sing.

"We should leave them," Aldrich whispered, beckoning. "She will call her mate’s fleeing spirit back into his body by singing his secret name, and no-one else must hear it.”

The Shee began to slip away by ones and twos, disappearing between the trees in a way that baffled the eyes.

“STOP!” Princess Mrouwl was imperious. “Our business is not yet concluded! You will guide us through these woods, past the Wizard-priests’ seminary and back out onto the ridgeway.”

“Ah well, you know there’s nothing I’d like better than to spend the time of day with you, but I’m a very busy person you understand and this encounter has cost me enough time already, so if you’ll excuse me I’ll just be about my busin ...”

“You will guide us,” said the cat, slowly and clearly, “or my friend will be forced to speak your secret name .... loudly!”

“I have no choice then, do I?” The elf pushed up the sleeves of his red jacket and held out his arms. He made a rapid series of gestures during which the Magician could have sworn that one hand passed clean through the other.

The two companions stood on a hilltop above a belt of ancient woodland. The path in front of them led somewhat to the left of the sun which was sinking towards a group of burial mounds clustered on the horizon. They were alone.

“It’ll be dark before long,” observed the cat, “we should think about finding a place to spend the night.”

The Magician rubbed his chin thoughtfully. “If it’s all the same to you, I think I’d rather put some distance between us and those woods first!”

“You have a point there.”

“Princess?”

“Yes.”

“Thank you. You saved our lives back there. How come you knew so much about the elves, what did you call them? The Shee.”

“After the wizard-priests took you to their seminary, I had a long talk with Biddy. She told me a lot about this world and the creatures that live here. The Shee are one of the magical races that lived on this planet long before the humans evolved. Creatures like them are widespread throughout the universe."

"There aren't any on my world - at least I've never heard anyone talk about them."

"They don't live on my world either. At least, they don't live there now. There are stories about them from the time before our machine age. I wonder if magic and technology are incompatible."

"Perhaps one day they'll be forced to abandon this world too."

"Probably, if the humans here develop according to the norm. I hope there'll always be somewhere for the magical folk though."

The Magician smiled. "It's a big universe," he said.

A couple of miles further on they came upon the campfire. The wood had burned down to a glowing bed of embers and a large piece of meat was sizzling over them on a makeshift spit. A weasely looking man was hunkered down beside the fire, turning the spit.

"There are two more men in the bushes off to your left," hissed the cat.

"Hello my friend," called the stranger, "come and join me."

"Thank you," replied the Magician. "Will your two friends over there be joining us too?"

The stranger laughed. It wasn't a particularly reassuring sound. "Torbert, Raven, come on out," he shouted, "you've been spotted!" Two men emerged rather shamefacedly from the undergrowth. They wore sturdy leather helmets and their muscles suggested intensive training. They didn't look like bird-watchers.

"Torbert and Raven are my protectors," explained the weasely one, holding out a greasy hand. "My name's Dagan, I'm a trader. I deal in rare goods, special items obtained to order. Items like that staff you're carrying."

"Sorry," said the Magician. "I'm afraid that the staff isn't for sale."

"No," Dagan murmured, "I didn't really expect that it would be." He sliced a hunk of meat from the sizzling joint with a wicked looking knife and offered it to him. "But if you ever change your mind .... I'll give you a good price for it."

Torbert spat into the fire. "We could just take it off him," he observed.

"Torbert!" Dagan managed to look genuinely shocked. "What a dreadful thing to say! This man and his, er, pet are our guests. We must treat them with courtesy and consideration." He turned to the Magician, who was sniffing suspiciously at the meat he was still holding, untouched, in his fingers. "Please excuse my associate, he is new to this business."

"What was he before?" enquired the cat, of no-one in particular, "an Estate Agent?"

"It's probably not his staff anyhow!" Torbert grumbled. "If he's a real Wizard-priest, where's his robe? Eh? Eh?"

"Yeah!" agreed Raven. "He likely nicked it off've some poor bloke and now he's swannin' round pretendin' to be sumfink what he's not!"

"Amazing!" Dagan's voice took on a tone of heavy sarcasm. "Did you think of that all by yourselves?"

"Yer!" Raven managed to convey oceans of pride via that one short (and somewhat mangled) syllable.

"WELL, STOP IT!" Torbert and Raven cowered at Dagan's sudden verbal assault. "I don't pay you to think! No-one is ever going to pay you to think! I can't for the life of me work out what those helmets are supposed to be protecting!"

"Oh, that's an easy one boss!" Torbert glowed like an eight year old who has just worked out the answer to a question that has been baffling the rest of the remedial maths group. "They're to protect our b....." He paused, his wrinkled brow betraying the thought processes crawling through his overworked mind. "Oh! Yeah. I get it now. Um."

"Sorry about that." Dagan turned back to the Magician with a synthetic smile. "They're not very bright .... but I promised their poor dear mother, just before she passed away, that I'd look after them."

"But our Mum's not .. aaargh! Whatcher do that for?" Comprehension dawned belatedly on Torbert's face. He took off his helmet and held it against his chest with both hands.

"Mind you," Dagan spoke conspiratorially, "they do have a point there. You don't look much like a Wizard-priest really. Perhaps you wouldn't mind giving us a little demonstration of your powers?"

The Magician looked at the now cold lump of greasy meat with distaste. His back-pack jumped and a small voice cried, "Hungry! HUNGRY!" He undid the lace and pushed the meat through the opening. When he straightened up three faces were regarding him with puzzled stares. He decided not to enlighten them.

"A demonstration?" he queried, "what did you have in mind?"

"Oh, nothing major! Just a small evidence of your power, a little magical exhibition to entertain three lonely travellers. Anything really."

"What? Something like this perhaps?" The Magician pushed up his sleeves and turned slowly, his fingers splayed, showing that there was nothing in his hands.

"Oh no!" The Princess yawned. "Not the billiard ball trick again."

"Raven," said our hero in a commanding voice. "I think I've found out what your helmet is protecting!" He reached out and pulled off the helmet, then plunged his hand into it. From its greasy depths he produced an egg.

"Only one egg?" mused the cat. "What's interfering with your magic?"

"Here," breathed Raven wonderingly, "what was that doing in there?

The Magician sniffed the egg cautiously. "I don't know," he said, "but it's been in there a very long time!" He crumpled the egg in his fingers and then with a fan which appeared miraculously in the other hand he wafted the resultant white flakes into the air. They floated away on the evening breeze.

"Excellent! Wonderful!" Dagan did indeed seem to be deeply impressed by the old confetti egg trick. "Do you still want to try taking the staff away by force, Torbert?"

"Not me Guv! Sorry Your Honour! We didn't mean no harm ... honest!"

“Still,” said Dagan thoughtfully, “I don’t think you could work your magic on me.”

“I wonder why not?” The Magician pounced on the back of Dagan’s collar and produced another egg. He sniffed at it cautiously.

“Old, like the other one?” enquired Raven.

“No .... in fact I think this one’s about to crack!” The Magician tossed the egg into the heart of the fire where it exploded with a very satisfying bang, throwing hot ashes all around the clearing.

“I think on the whole that I preferred the billiard balls,” remarked the cat, peering around a tree some ten metres away.

Dagan brushed ash from his tunic. “You must be a very powerful wizard,” he mused.

“Why? because of the fireworks?”

“No! Because I’m wearing an iron knife!”

“Iron? I don’t think I understand.”

“Iron inhibits magic,” Dagan explained. “Only the most powerful magicians can overcome its effect.”

“It’s what we were saying earlier,” hissed the cat. “About magic and technology being incompatible.”

“If you’re that powerful,” Dagan continued, “you could challenge the Arch Magician or whatever they call him, and take over as boss of all the Wizard-priests.”

“I already did that.” the Magician said without thinking.

“Then .... you must be the new Arch-whatsit?”

“No. I gave him his job back.”

“You gave him his job back?” Dagan was obviously having trouble understanding. “Why would you give back the most powerful position in the whole of this part of the world?”

“I didn’t want all that power,” explained the Magician. “Besides, it seemed to be the will of the Sky Father.”

Dagan was shaking his head from side to side. "You beat him in a magical contest, and then you gave him his job back? He must really hate you."

"No." A silly idea had just suggested itself to the Magician and he was beginning to enjoy himself. "We're the best of friends, old Ligulf and I."

"Er boss?"

"Shut up Raven. Did you say ... Ligulf?"

"Boss .... if you know someone's real name ..."

"Shut up Raven!"

"But it gives you power over ..."

"Shut up, shut up, shut up!"

"That's right," confirmed the Magician with a smile, "Ligulf. It means fiery wolf or something of the sort. He's a nice guy is old Ligulf. He gave me this staff you know. Of course he's got a much finer one. You should see the quality of the inlays - remarkable craftsmanship."

"Er, boss?"

"Shut up Torbert! Er, it's been a real pleasure meeting you Mr ... er, I mean, er, friend. We mustn't detain you any longer. Come on Torbert, come on Raven - we have an appointment to keep. Goodbye!"

With this the unsavoury trio rushed off into the gathering darkness, in the general direction of the seminary. The Magician stood and watched them until they were out of sight, his shoulders shaking with silent mirth.

"I take it," the cat enquired, "that they are going to the seminary to relieve the Arch-mage of his staff?"

"I should think so, yes."

"And they believe that they will be protected by their knowledge of his secret name?"

"That's about the size of it."

"The secret name which is Ligulf?"

“I wouldn’t know,” the Magician giggled. “It’s a secret!”

“Usually,” said the cat, “I have a lot of trouble understanding the human concept of humour, but in this case I have to admit ... that’s enough to make a cat laugh!”

The Magician took a deep breath and let it out slowly. “ They’ve left their fire and their supper,” he said. I think this might be a good place to settle down for the night.”

Chapter 22

The village lying below them was a hive of activity. A bunch of three men were vigorously cleansing the animal pens. Another group were hammering in fence posts and erecting wattle panels, whilst a third squad were toiling in the bottom of the perimeter ditch, making it deeper and wider. Two brave individuals were up on the roof of one of the houses, tying down bundles of reeds and two more were chopping up a pile of firewood that, in another time and place, would have kept a good-sized power station going for a couple of weeks.

Something was missing. The Magician surveyed the activity for a while and tried to put his finger on it.

"Why are they all so quiet?" asked the cat.

That was it! So many men, all working hard on shared projects and yet, there was no conversation, no friendly banter - and no laughter.

The two companions strolled down the hill and into the village. They stopped beside one of the houses. Sitting just outside was a strapping great giant of a man with bulging biceps. The Magician decided that his physique and the leather apron he was wearing probably marked him out as the village bronze smith. Cradled in his lap was a large bronze cooking pot which gleamed in the sunlight. Despite this, he was scrubbing at it with a mixture of sand and water as though he meant to rub a hole in it.

"Good morning," said the Magician affably, "can you tell me the name of this village?"

"Shhh!" The smith looked up at him and scowled. He noticed the staff. "Oh! Er, no offence meant, you understand? It's just that 'er in the 'ouse don't 'old with me chatting when I've got work to do."

"Which is all the time nowadays," he added bitterly.

"Red!" A querulous voice issued from the open door. "Don't you start nattering to that worthless layabout Todd from next door! If you've got time to talk, you've got time to come in here and scrub the hearth!"

Red's voice took on a pleading tone. "I'm not talking to Todd, my love. We 'ave...," he looked again at the staff the magician was leaning on, "an important visitor to the village!"

The voice of 'er in the 'ouse might have thawed by an unmeasurable fraction of a degree. "Well alright, but don't think you can spend the rest of the day entertaining visitors, there's still plenty of pots to clean!"

"Yes dear, - thank you dear." The giant bowed his head and muttered something unintelligible into his beard. He went back to scrubbing viciously at the pot.

"Erhum," the Magician coughed, " ... the name of this village?"

"Oh yeah! This 'ere is the village of Stoneford," Red told him, "and you're welcome to it!"

Red's better half appeared at the doorway. "I thought I told you.. ," she began. Her eyes took in the strange couple standing outside her home. The enormous golden-furred cat was certainly unusual and more than a little intimidating, but the real eye-opener was the tall man with the foreign looks. His staff proclaimed him to be a Wizard-priest, but his outlandish clothes made him seem infinitely more mysterious.

Unconsciously, she smoothed her skirt and stood a little straighter. Her chin (and her chest) lifted and her pupils widened. "Well, hello!" she husked. "It's so nice to see a real man around this village!"

Red's lips tightened into a narrow line, contrasting with the slack-jawed gape that dominated the face of the bemused Magician.

"For crying out loud," Mrouwl hissed, "shut your mouth. You look like a complete idiot! Why is this woman giving you totally different status from her husband? Get us invited in and let's find out what's going on here."

"Er, hello," the Magician muttered, "We've ah, come a long way looking for some information. I wonder, could we come in and talk to you?"

"Both!" hissed the cat.

"Er, yes ... talk to you both."

Red’s wife brushed her hair back with splayed fingers and tilted her head slightly. “Why, that would be lovely,” she said. Please come in and sit down. Red! Make our visitors some tea.”

It took some time to make everyone comfortable. Mrouwl persuaded the Magician to ask for a bowl of milk. The kitten promptly woke up and fell into the bowl. Eventually he was cleaned up and settled himself down in the Magician’s lap.

Over the next forty minutes, the Magician drank two mugs of mediocre tea and learned all about the happenings of the previous week. The men of Stoneford had straggled back from their abortive raiding party dirty, smelly, injured, hung-over and dispirited. They had lost all of their self-confidence, all of their machismo.

At that critical time the women folk had moved against them like a well-drilled military assault force. Before they knew what was happening, the demoralised men found themselves separated from their friends, dominated and conquered. Jobs that had been waiting for years were getting done, a sure sign that there had been a change in the social order.

“It was all the fault of that blonde vixen,” Red gritted. “She’s some sort of evil spirit, that’s what she is.”

“Blonde you say? Tall with blue eyes and an irresistible smile?”

“Don’t talk to me about that smile! It was that smile that made our leaders walk into ‘er trap. One flash of that blasted smile and they went to pieces!”

The Magician leapt to his feet and playfully punched the nearest wooden upright. “Yippee! Ouch! It’s her! Mrouwl - we’ve found Gloria!”

Red’s wife looked at him in amazement. “You’re looking for her?” she demanded. “Whatever for? Why would a Wizard-priest be looking for a witch?”

“Because,” he was gathering up his belongings, eager to set out on the final leg of his journey, “I’m going to marry her, that’s why.”

“You’re mad,” Red opined, making the sign against the evil eye. “You don’t marry a woman like that. You admire ‘er, sure.” A thoughtful look passed across his face. “You dream about ‘er for the rest of your life, maybe.” He seemed not to notice the increasingly annoyed expression on his wife’s face. “But you don’t marry ‘er. In fact, you spend the rest of your days hoping that no poor beggar ever has to actually marry ‘er. ‘Appiness,” he theorized, “is not marrying a woman like that!”

Red’s lady poked him in the chest with an outstretched finger. She was a good head shorter than he, roughly half his mass and although wiry, could never have matched his strength. He cowered. “Now listen to me Red! I won’t have you looking at other women like that - or dreaming about them either! You behave yourself, do you hear me? As for this gentleman, if he thinks that she’ll marry him then good luck to him!”

She turned to the Magician with a puzzled frown. “Though if I might make so bold sir, how does a gentleman like you come to fall in love with a woman like her?”

“Oh, that’s no puzzle, she’s been my assistant for years.”

“Your ...... assistant?” It was dawning on Red that this stranger was claiming that he was the boss, the superior, the employer of the woman who had been the nemesis of every man in the village.

The significance of the statement hadn’t been lost on Mrs Red either. “Now then,” she said, bustling towards the door. “We mustn’t keep Mr ... er ... this gentleman any longer. It’s been very nice I’m sure, but you’ll be wanting to get along, won’t you? Do please call again. Goodbye.”

“Actually,” a mischievous smile touched the Magician’s lips as he tucked the kitten back into his bag, “I was rather hoping that your husband would consent to guide me at least part of the way?”

“I’m sure that on any other day he would have loved to, but he has so much to do, and he really can’t spare the time to .....”

The firm voice of the village bronze smith interrupted her in mid-denial. “I’d be glad to come along,” he said. “Just give me a moment to grab a jug of ale. It’s a warm day and the walk’ll make us thirsty.” He turned to his wife, a new confidence growing behind his eyes. “I’ll be back for tea love. Why don't you make that stew of yours with the dumplings - you know I like that."

She looked at him for a moment. Their relationship had changed again, and this time there'd be respect on both sides. "Get along with you then," she smiled, "I'll make you something nice."

It was about four kilometres from Stoneford to Muddybrook as the crow flew. Following the line of the river made the journey rather longer and it was well past mid-day when the trio waded across the ford and trudged up the track to the village gate.

The Magician was suffering from a sense of déja vu. In the middle of the compound a couple of men were whitewashing a henhouse. An old chap wearing a pinny was hanging washing on a line strung between two of the houses and in a small compound abutting the perimeter fence a big fellow was attempting to fasten an enormous wooden wheel to an ox cart.

The kitten struggled out of the bag and, after a complicated sequence of stretches, went off for a look around.

"Strewth!" Red was impressed. "She's done it 'ere an' all!" Mindful of recent events in his own village he crept up to the oldster with the washing basket and lowered his voice to a whisper. "Got you at it too 'ave they?" he asked sympathetically.

"Eh?" The old fellow put a cupped hand to his ear and wrinkled up his face in concentration. "You'll 'ave to speak up a bit young man, I'm rather hard of hearing, you know? What can I do for you?"

"We're looking for a woman," Red informed him.

"The old chap cackled. "So were that lot who came 'ere last week," he grinned. "They got quite a shock, let me tell you!"

"What my friend means to say," explained the Magician coming to the rescue, "is that we're looking for a particular woman, a close personal friend of mine. She's tall, blonde and has a devastating smile."

"Oh! You mean Gloria."

"Yes," Red looked thoughtful. "Gloria." He glanced around nervously and licked his lips.

"She's not 'ere."

"Not here?" The Magician was stricken. "But I thought you said ..."

"Oh, don't you worry young feller. She lives 'ere all right. That's her house over there, or at least the one she shares with old Meg. Meg's our village witch you know ... or at least, she was. I'm not sure any more."

"But if she's not here, where would I find her?"

"They've gone on an outing. Would you believe it? They've packed themselves a picnic and gone off sightseeing!"

The kitten came tearing round the outside of the building and skidded to a halt between the Magician's feet. As he reached down to pick up the trembling creature, the largest of the village dogs, a shaggy coated monster with near terminal halitosis, swaggered round the corner hot on the trail of the kitten. It found itself face to face with Mrouwl. It involuntarily took a complicated four-footed step backwards and gulped. From the impenetrable depths[1] of its doggy brain, an instinctive behaviour suggested itself. "Woof?" it offered, "woof, WOOF!"

Mrouwl stiffened. All of the hair on her back and tail stood on end. She laid her ears back flat to her skull and her lips peeled back, revealing a mouthful of teeth that wouldn't have disgraced a shark. She hissed loudly. The dog back-pedalled frantically. In its hurry to escape it tripped over its own back paws and sprawled in the mud. The next moment it was gone, running flat out with its tail between its legs.

The Princess smoothed down her fur and sat down. "I know it's hardly dignified to frighten such primitive creatures," she admitted, "but it is such fun!"

The Magician turned to the old laundryman. "You were saying," he prompted, "something about an outing?"

---

[1]All right then - shallows.

“Right you are young sir, I was that. Well, when Miss Gloria found out that we all have to go and work on the big temple once a year, she wanted to see it. Of course, we told ‘er that females weren’t allowed up there, but the more we told ‘er it wasn’t allowed, the more determined she got. In the end she persuaded all the women folk that they ought to see where their men were going off to, and they organized this ‘ere outing. There’ll be ‘ell to pay when your lot realize what’s going on.”

“My lot? What do you mean, my lot?”

“Why, the Wizard-priests, sir. That is what your staff means isn’t it?”

“Oh, good grief!” The Magician had finally made all the connections. “The Archmage‘ll be livid. He might do anything! I’ve got to get there as fast as possible. Red - would you ask that man over there if we could borrow his ox cart?”

Chapter 23

The babble of gossip and laughter gradually died away. Gloria tore her attention away from her third ham sandwich and looked up. The stone circle that surrounded them was itself surrounded by a grim faced ring of wizard-priests. Each one wore the traditional long grey robe, the rope belt and the wickedly sharp bronze knife of office. Each also carried a staff of hard wood, intricately carved and decorated with metal and bone inlays. The circle parted and a priest stepped through the gap. He was bearded and robed like the others, but his robes were white, the first real white that Gloria had seen since arriving on this planet. The thought that he was about to declare some sort of washing powder doorstep challenge flitted through her mind and she smiled involuntarily. She was still smiling as she rose gracefully to meet him, brushing a few crumbs from her skirt.

The Archmage knew exactly how this meeting was going to proceed. He would shout and threaten a little, perhaps throw around some magical fireworks to underline his annoyance at finding these inferiors in his Henge, and then the wizard-priests would allow the women to make a run for it, dealing them a few cracks across their heads and backs with their staffs on the way. Honour would have been satisfied, male superiority would have been re-asserted and everyone could get on with business as usual.

He pulled himself up to his full majestic height, raised his arms and took a deep breath, drawing upon the vocal training he had undergone in bardic school as a boy. Then he noticed Gloria's smile. It hit him like a punch in the solar plexus. The wind whistled out of his lungs.

"What you doin' ere?" he wheezed.

"Didn't anyone tell you?" Gloria's smile wouldn't let go of his eyes. "It's a W.I. picnic!"

"W.I.?"

"Witches Institute! You shouldn't be here you know, it's a women only organization. Still, we don't want to be anti-social. Sit down and have a rock cake. They're really delicious, Sister Mabel made them."

The Archmage still seemed to be having trouble with his breathing. One of the ladies handed him a beaker of tea. He had taken a couple of sips of the milky herb infusion before he realised what he was doing.

"But," he said, "but, but .... you're in our henge dammit!" Out of the corner of his eye, he could see brother Bloodmoon appreciatively munching an enormous rock cake.

"You've got to understand," he pleaded, "this place is sacred to the Sky God. Any female intrusion into this place is a desecration, an insult to the God himself."

"Nonsense!" Gloria was having none of it. "I know what happens at your midsummer solstice celebrations!"

The Archmage turned the colour of a ripe tomato. "You do?" he squeaked. He cleared his throat and tried again. "You do?"

"Of course," said Gloria. "It's fertility symbolism."

"Oh," said the venerable wizard-priest, looking somewhat relieved, "that!"

"The tall stone outside the main circle," Gloria explained, "is a phallic symbol, of course. But at the midsummer solstice something very impressive happens. As the sun rises over the horizon, the stone casts a long shadow right through the entrance of the henge and into the smaller group of stones that stand at the very centre. The shadowy phallus of the Sky God penetrates the body of the Earth Mother, ensuring fertility for another year. Then, as the sun climbs higher into the sky it shrinks away, just like any other male organ after the main event."

"Well, of course you're right," admitted the Archmage, accepting a cheese sandwich, "but surely if you understand all of that, you can see that this is no place for females to be."

"No," said Gloria, "I can't! If this place is the vulva of the Earth Mother, then it is an essentially female place, and <u>you</u> are the interloper!"

"Can I top up your tea, Archmage?" said a voice.

"Thank you very much," the Archmage replied absently. He held out his beaker, looked up and froze. Standing in front of him, holding a large cauldron of freshly brewed herb tea and a milk jug was .... Brother Deepstone!

"Hang on one blasted minute," said the old one through clenched teeth. "What the blistering blue blazes do you think you're doing?"

"Er, well," the Brotherhood's chief enforcer had the guilty look of a guard dog caught having his tummy tickled by a burglar. "It's a very heavy cauldron, and Daphne seemed to be having trouble with it, so I just thought ....." His voice trailed away into embarrassed silence.

"Daphne!" snarled the Archmage. "Tea! Rock cakes! Cheese sandwiches! Sitting around on the grass enjoying a picnic inside our own henge, with, with, ... with a bunch of flaming witches! We've been ruddy well subverted!"

In a matter of moments the situation had changed beyond all hope of recognition. A battle line had been drawn. On one side were Gloria and her new found friends, the hitherto downtrodden witches. On the other side were the accustomed rulers of this world's magical realm, the Wizard-priests. Both groups had fallen naturally into that defensive crouch habitually adopted by all devotees of Far Eastern martial arts - and eight year olds in the school playground.

The Archmage stepped forward. He was flanked by brothers Deepstone and Bloodmoon. He pointed an imperious finger at the assembled members of Muddybrook W.I. "I abjure and conjure you," he intoned, "by all the foul heresies of your infernal doctrine, to get thee hence from this place and never to return, under pain of eternal dissolution."

"Oooh, get 'im!" came a voice from the opposing ranks. "Don't he talk lovely!"

"No, no ... even now control your righteous anger," the Archmage told his uncomprehending troops. "Let it be recorded in the annals of our noble brotherhood that we gave these mere females every opportunity to escape the awful fate that they so richly deserve. I shall count to ten. One, ... two, ... "

“’Ere, look , I hope this countin’ ain't goin’ to take too long, only I got to pick up the kids from the child minder at five o’clock, so could we get on wiv it?”

“three, ...four, ... five, ...”

“Per’aps we ought ter sit down and get comfterble ..... I reckon he’s still got ter think o’ sommat ter do when he gets ter ten.”

“ six, ...seven, ... ”

“I challenge you,” said Gloria, spoiling a couple of side bets that the old fellow probably couldn’t count as far as ten anyway.

eight, ...nine, ... er, what?”

“I challenge you.”

“Oh no,” muttered Brother Bloodmoon, “not again!”

“You can’t challenge me.” The rules were very clear in his mind, after all he’d only just undergone a very disquieting refresher course. “Only a man may challenge for the position of Archmage, for which you should be grateful, since the fate of the loser is to be joined with the spirit of the Sky Father.”

“I don’t want to be Arch-whatsit.”

“Well, if you don’t want my job, what do you want?”

Gloria’s eyes twinkled. “I want your henge!”

In any half decent medical facility, the Archmage would have been immediately diagnosed as a chronic asthmatic. He gasped and wheezed. “You .... hurgh, you want my .... whoof, ... my henge .... aaargh?" He allowed himself to be led aside and seated comfortably.

Gloria’s voice was gentle as she handed him a drink. “I don’t want to take it away from you,” she conceded, “I just want the witches to have the right to share it with you.”

“Sh ... share? Hurgh! You want to ... whoof .... share?” His breathing was easing. “Impossible! Our two faiths may co-exist .... huff .... but they are not compatible!” He looked around and realized that he had been seated on, of all things, the altar stone. He sprang to his feet, thereby sending himself into a relapse.

Gloria was sympathetic, but uncompromising. “If you won’t share voluntarily,” she told him, “then you must accept my challenge.”

“What .... herph .... what is the nature of your .... whooo, challenge?”

She stood quietly for a few moments, considering. “You claim that the Sky Father is all powerful,” she said slowly. “My friends the witches make the same claim for the Earth Mother. I propose a trial of power. We’ll build a big bonfire. The side whose magic lights the fire in spite of the other side’s disbelief is the winner. O.K?”

The Archmage took a deep breath. He straightened up until he was almost looking her in the eye. “I accept,” he said. “On one condition. If you lose, as you surely will, you and all your witches will leave this place and will never, ever return.”

“You have my word,” said Gloria.

It didn’t take long to build the bonfire, since there was no shortage of willing helpers. By mutual agreement it was piled up to the Northeast of the Henge, beside the avenue which ran from the Temple to a group of burial mounds near the river.

“You can go first.” Gloria needed time to think. For all her outward show of aplomb, she still didn’t have a clue how she was going to pull this off. Meg raised her hand and all the members of Muddybrook W.I. began to radiate disbelief. They were good at it.[1]

The Archmage strode forward confidently. He levelled his staff at the mound of timber and said something that Gloria’s translator implant gave up on.

Nothing happened.

He looked at his staff. He hefted it in his hand. Brothers Deepstone and Bloodmoon both started towards him, but he waved them back. “Don’t worry lads,” he said jovially, “I’m not going to do anything like that again!” He turned to his opponent. “Your disbelief is strong,” he admitted. “You don’t have a brother by any chance?”

---

[1]Disbelief is a state of mind that comes easily to most women. Ask anyone who’s tried to tell his wife that he’s two hours late for dinner because of leaves on the railway line!

"No," she shook her head slowly, "I'm an only child. Why do you ask?"

"Oh, it just occurred to me." He turned to the assembled Wizard-priests. "I need your strength, my brothers. Merge your concentration with mine, and we will overcome this female resolve." He turned back to the unlit fire. "And now," .... something was trying to draw itself to his attention. It was niggling away at the back of his mind, spoiling his concentration. It was something that he'd seen. No! It couldn't be! He turned around slowly, fervently praying that he was mistaken. Standing between Bloodmoon and Deepstone, a friendly smile on his face and a Wizard's staff in his hand, was the Magician.

"Hello," he said. "How are things? That's a nice knife you're wearing!"

The Archmage could feel his chest beginning to tighten again. "Wha ... what are you doing here?"

"It's a long story," the Magician temporised. "I'll tell you all about it later. Just carry on and I'll try not to get in the way." He winked at Gloria and was warmed by her answering smile.

That smile affected more than one man in the assembled ranks. Concentration didn't so much waver as completely fall apart. The Archmage's incendiary spell failed again. He hurled his staff to the ground and jumped on it. "All right," he snarled, "it's your turn!"

Gloria rushed to the Magician. She threw her arms around him and hugged him tight. Deep sighs could be heard from both groups. She appeared to be nibbling his ear! "Quick," she whispered, "which pocket is your Helvetian space-navy penknife in?"

"The right-hand jacket pocket," he felt her hand slip down over his ribs, "but there's something you should know."

"Not now *The*."

"This is important."

"No time, tell me later."

The assembled witches cheered as Gloria strode towards the bonfire. The face of every Wizard-priest was screwed up in concentration as he tried to negate her magic with disciplined disbelief. The Magician's knuckles were white as he gripped his staff.

Gloria stopped in front of the pile of wood. She turned to face the onlookers. “Earth Mother,” she cried, “Accept the homage of your disciples!” As the witches echoed her shout, she plunged her hand into the pile. At once flames burst around her arm. Within seconds the pile of wood was burning fiercely. A groan went up from the ranks of the Wizard-priests.

The flickering light penetrated the Magician’s tightly closed eyes. He stole a quick glance. Hand in hand, the witches were dancing around the fire. The Archmage was slumped in the middle of a group of brothers. He pointed at the Magician. “This is your fault,” he shouted.

“No, not my fault.” The magician’s voice was firm. “ - Yours! It’s time to think again. There’s strength in unity you know. Think about it.”

Gloria whirled out of the dance and he caught her up in his arms. “Thank you *The*,” she said. “I didn’t know what I was going to do! Without the laser igniter on your space-navy penknife I’d have lost the contest.”

“No,” he replied thoughtfully, “I don’t think you would have.”

Gloria looked hard at her man. “What are you trying to tell me?”

“Exactly what I tried to tell you when you took it from my pocket. The power source in my penknife exhausted itself a fortnight ago. You lit that bonfire all by yourself. It’s just as Betel said. You only have to believe.” He whirled her off into the dance.

Elsewhere in the crowd, Bloodmoon found himself dancing with a generously endowed lady who clasped him amorously to her ample bosom as they threaded their way among the other revellers.

“Oooh! Don’t you dance lovely?” she sighed. “I didn’t know you Wizard-priests went in fer dancin’.”

Bloodmoon’s eyes went misty with recollected happiness. “I wasn’t always a member of this order,” he admitted, “once upon a time I knew how to party!”

The long blonde eyelashes fluttered in a parody of innocent shyness. “Yer full of surprises,” she opined. “What’s yer name then?”

“Bloodmoon ...... what’s yours ...... beautiful?”

“Goldy.”

“Goldy. What a lovely name. Goldy .... Goldy? Not, not er, Goldy B-B-B-Bedstraw?”

“Yeah, that’s me dearie! Goldy Bedstraw!” She looked around in obvious puzzlement. “’Ere. Where’d ‘ee go then?”

Chapter 24

The stars were out long before the revellers made it back to Muddybrook. The Magician and Gloria stood with their arms around each other, looking at the unfamiliar constellations, and dreaming of a life together under these skies.

“A credit for them,” murmured the happiest man in the world.

“I beg your pardon?”

“Your thoughts. I was offering a credit for them.”

“Oh! You’ll be disappointed. I was wondering why that star is flashing.”

The Magician followed her outstretched arm. “Where? Oh yes, I can see it. It’s moving relative to the other stars.” He spun her around. “Gloria! It’s a space ship. It must be in orbit. I think the rescue mission has finally arrived!”

Another voice purred in the darkness. “So you’ve finally noticed have you? They’ve been calling us for the past fifteen minutes.”

“Calling us?” The Magician was puzzled. “How have they been calling us?”

“On my communicator of course. What did you think this is around my neck - an address tag?”

Gloria clapped her hands together. “Oh I’m so glad for you Mrouwl! Have you called them back yet?”

“It’s not quite that easy,” the Princess replied. “Batteries would give a tiny device like this almost no worthwhile operational life. It is designed to draw power from a wide range of available energy sources. At the moment it is drawing on my body heat, which is sufficient to receive the relatively powerful signals coming from the rescue ship. However, to transmit a reply would use much more energy. I shall need your help.”

“I’m afraid I don’t know much about technology,” Gloria admitted, “still, what will you need?”

"Lots of boiling water."

The Magician grinned. "You didn't say you were going to have kittens. Who's the lucky Tom?"

Mrouwl rested her head against Gloria's leg for a moment. "I don't know how you put up with him," she growled.

It took ages to coax the fire in Gloria's hut back to life, and even longer to boil the enormous bronze cauldron full of water. Even so, the skies were still dark when the three castaways finally established two-way contact with the Galactic Patrol and Protection Vessel *Knight Errant.*

It was soon established that a landing strip of some description would be needed so that a shuttlecraft could land conveniently close to their location. Gloria was the first to think of a solution.

"To the north of the temple!" she shouted. "There's a long narrow enclosure, with a ditch all round it. Some sort of parade ground, or race course or something. If we cleaned up the ditch, the white chalk would make an outline for the pilot to aim for - and we could clear away all the loose stones inside it so that he can land and take off safely."

Work began the next day. The men from the two villages cleaned out the ditch, piling the chalky spoil into a rampart that outlined the landing strip in gleaming white. The women walked the two and three-quarters of a kilometre in line abreast, putting small stones into baskets which were emptied into the ditch. It was the first time that men and women alike had worked together on a shared project of this scale, and an almost holiday atmosphere characterized the five days of communal labour. Children played happily all over the site, and folk from both communities made new friends, sharing picnic meals and working shoulder to shoulder.

On the last day, the wizard-priests came from the seminary to bless the work, and stayed to entertain the children and adults with some magical fireworks. Betel juggled and cracked jokes and there was music and dancing far into the night.

Chapter 25

The landing strip was barely long enough. The landing craft bucked and jolted along it, threatening all the time to veer off into the surrounding scrub, and eventually slowed to a halt less than a fuselage's length from the end of the cleared area. Its skin, superheated by atmospheric entry, clicked and popped as it began to cool.

The four castaways, accompanied by Meg, the Archmage and Bryony, walked up to it cautiously.

"HELLO THERE." The rusty voice emanated from a grill near the hatch. "I'M GLAD TO SEE YOU ALL LOOKING SO WELL."

Betel groaned. "You didn't by any chance have a brother?" he enquired. "Unreasonably cheerful in the face of disaster?"

"IN A MANNER OF SPEAKING, SIR. YOU SEE IN A SENSE ALL COMPUTERS ARE, SO TO SPEAK, ELEMENTS OF A MUCH LARGER SUPERCOMPUTER, WHICH IS SIMULTANEOUSLY EVERYWHERE AND NOWHERE."

"You sound just like him," Betel gritted. "Chatty and yet totally uninformative at the same time!"

"I WAS AFRAID THAT YOU WOULDN'T GET FAR ENOUGH AWAY BEFORE THE ENGINES OVERLOADED, SIR. AS I RECALL, YOUR FRIEND HAD TO CARRY YOU."

"It's him!" Betel hissed through clenched teeth. "It's that blasted computer again! How can that be? I thought he burned up with the shuttle!"

The Magician's brow uncreased fractionally. "I think I understand some of this," he announced. "If all the computers in explored space share the same database and programs, then in a sense they are all elements of one massive, parallel processing supercomputer?"

"THAT'S IT EXACTLY, SIR."

"So when we talk to you, if you share his memories and programming, we are also talking to the escape craft computer?"

"IF I MAY SAY SO, SIR, YOU HAVE A FINE GRASP OF LOGICAL THOUGHT."

Betel was still puzzled. "So how did that memory about you carrying me get into his skull - or whatever it is that he uses for one?"

The Magician clicked his fingers and smiled. "The light show!" he said. "We thought that the, what did he call it? Oh yes, pulse of coherent light, was just an S.O.S. beacon. It wasn't, was it? It must have been a final upload of all the data in our computer's memory banks."

"BRAVO, SIR."

Betel glared at the speaker grill. "You may know a lot of stuff," he said, "but it still takes a human being to explain it clearly!"

"THANK YOU, SIR. AND NOW MAY I REQUEST THAT YOU STAND BACK? I HAVE JUST RECEIVED AN INSTRUCTION FROM INSIDE THE CRAFT TO OPEN THE HATCH."

The heavy hatch thunked onto the grass, obliterating Betel's most recent footprints. He glared at it.

A Space Marine Lieutenant in full-dress uniform marched smartly down the ramp. He brushed past Betel and the Magician and came to ramrod straight attention in front of the Princess. His arm sprang into a quivering salute. "Your Royal Highness!" he barked. "The Captain and crew request the pleasure of your company aboard the Galactic Patrol and Protection Vessel *Knight Errant*."

"HUNGRY," a small voice interrupted from somewhere below the level of the Lieutenant's disciplined stare. He was aware of a disturbance at trouser turnup level.

Betel sniggered. The officer's hitherto spotless dress trousers were being covered in a layer of tabby hairs as the kitten, having escaped from Bryony's arms, attempted to make a new friend - hopefully one with some food to spare.

Mrouwl carefully ignored the incident. "I assume that your kind invitation includes my friends?" she purred.

"I am sorry Your Highness," he said. "I have no instructions regarding the embarkation of additional personnel at this time. The invitation is specifically for yourself and relates to a party that is being given in the wardroom to celebrate your rescue."

"You mean we're not allowed on board?" Betel asked incredulously.

"I am very sorry sir," the officer didn't look sorry at all. "My orders are that only the Princess Mrouwl shall be allowed to board this vehicle."

"You didn't have a brother on board the Gigantean, did you?"

"I'm sorry sir, I don't think I understand."

"No." Betel shook his head. "I don't suppose you do, at that."

"AHEM!" A RUSTY VOICE CRACKLED ABOVE BETEL'S HEAD. "DON'T WORRY, SIR. YELLOW STAR LINES NEVER ABANDONS A PASSENGER. THE RESCUE SKIFF WILL BE ALONG IN A COUPLE OF YEARS."

"You don't understand!" Betel hissed at the grill. "I don't want to be rescued. I like it here. I just don't like the thought of being abandoned!"

The cat yawned and stretched. She stood up and walked towards the ramp. "Stand aside Lieutenant," she growled. "My friends and I are going to a party."

As the bemused officer watched open-mouthed, Mrouwl paced up the ramp, the kitten dancing playfully around her. Gloria and Meg strolled into the craft, chatting amiably and followed by Betel and Bryony, hand in hand. The Magician turned to the Archmage and raised an eyebrow. The old man smiled. He gestured at Gloria's retreating back. "If she dares to fly into the Sky God's domain," he said, "then so do I!"

Chapter 26

The party had been a great success. The food (replicated, but still accurately reproducing the delicacies of a dozen planets) was delicious and the supply of drink was seemingly inexhaustible. The Magician and Betel had been persuaded to perform for the most appreciative of audiences. Too appreciative.

“You realize, of course, that we can’t let you go back down there?”

“Now see here, Captain,” Betel was once again becoming frustrated with the logic of officialdom.[1]

“No. Mr ... er ... Betel? You see here. That planet down there is off limits. It is designated as such by the **C**onfederation **O**rganization for the **P**roper **P**rotection of **E**volving **R**aces with **S**apience. There must be no interference with the society of that world.”

“No interference?” The Magician was smiling wryly. “You’ve landed a military shuttlecraft on a landing strip right next to their largest religious monument. You’ve kidnapped three of their people, one of whom is the most important religious leader in this hemisphere, and you claim to be avoiding interference? What are you going to tell the COPPERS?”

The Captain pursed his lips. “I must remind you sir, that my officer attempted to prevent your uninvited visit to this vessel. If you had stayed on the surface with your new found friends, much of this unpleasantness could have been avoided.” He gestured to two burly crewmen who were standing nearby. “Kindly conduct our guests to their quarters,” he said, “and lock them in.”

The Archmage stepped forward. “Taste the wrath of the Sky God,” he snarled and pointing his staff at the Captain he said something that brought a blush to Bryony’s cheek.

Nothing happened.

---

[1]A concept as unreal as ‘Military Intelligence’, ‘common sense’ or ‘Freedom of Information’!

"Oh, for crying out loud!" breathed the enraged ancient. "Are you all wizards?"

"It's all this iron around us," explained the Magician as they were hustled off the bridge and down a narrow corridor. "It inhibits magic."

"Iron inhibits magic?" The old fellow's brain was churning furiously. "Like this iron knife I'm wearing?"

"Are you?" The Magician tried to look surprised. "Where did you get that from?"

"Never mind that. I've just worked out why I couldn't light that blasted bonfire!"

Gloria took his hand. "Try not to be too angry," she murmured.

"Angry? I'm not angry! I'm delighted! For a while there I thought I was losing my touch!"

"Here we are then." The crewman on the left held open a door. "Gents in here and ladies next door if you please. I'll take that wicked looking knife if you don't mind Sir?"

The Archmage grimaced as he pulled the knife from his belt. "Look upon it as a present," he said. "I won't be wanting it back."

Before the door had slammed, Betel was sitting on the bottom bunk, looking quizzically at his friend. "What do we do now?" he asked.

"Gentlemen," smiled the Magician, ferreting around in one of his many pockets for a piece of wire, "the prison that can hold me has not yet been built." He inserted the wire into the lock and began to wiggle it around. There was a blinding flash and the door slid into the wall. "Now for the ladies," he said. As he bent towards the lock of the next cabin, there was another eye-searing flash. He was still blinking rapidly when Gloria stepped through the door holding one of Meg's bronze hairpins.

"Come on," said Gloria, "we've got to get to the escape craft before anyone notices that we're free."

A klaxon sounded and the tannoy began to blare. "SECURITY ALERT. SECURITY ALERT. UNAUTHORIZED EXIT FROM DETENTION CABINS ON DECK C."

Betel glared at the speaker grill above his head. "Traitor," he snarled.

"OH, HELLO SIR. THERE IS A SECURITY PROBLEM ON THIS DECK. FOR YOUR OWN SAFETY, MAY I RECOMMEND THAT YOU AND YOUR FRIENDS MOVE TO A LESS DANGEROUS LOCATION?"

"A good idea," said the Magician, wondering if it was possible that the computer really hadn't been told who the occupants of the detention cabins were. "We were ready to leave anyway. Could you direct us to the landing craft?"

"MY PLEASURE SIR. PLEASE FOLLOW THE RED ARROWS ON THE CORRIDOR FLOOR."

Betel grimaced. "I don't care what happens," he declared, "nothing will ever get me into one of those plastic beach balls again!"

"Don't worry," The Magician was grinning, "we're all staying together this time."

The red arrows led the fugitives to a pair of lift doors which whooshed open as they approached.

"PLEASE STEP INSIDE," SAID THE COMPUTER. "THIS LIFT WILL TAKE YOU TO LANDING CRAFT BAY NUMBER 1."

"You wouldn't lie to us would you?" Betel asked suspiciously.

"MY PROGRAMMING SPECIFICALLY PRECLUDES ME FROM DELIBERATELY IMPARTING FLAWED OR ERRONEOUS DATA SIR."

Betel looked at Gloria. "What did he say?"

"He said his answers are always truthful," said Gloria, stepping into the lift. "I just hope we've asked all the right questions."

The lift dropped like a stone. Red numbers on the control panel rolled over faster and faster. It slowed and stopped. The computer had not lied. As the doors opened, the words 'LANDING CRAFT BAY NUMBER 1' could be clearly seen stencilled across the opposite wall. A gleaming silver landing craft filled half of the cavernous space. Standing in front of it were the Captain and a squad of space marines.

Gloria sighed. "I've just thought of a question we should have asked," she murmured.

"Computer!" The Magician was the first to react. "Close the lift doors. Get us out of here."

"I AM SORRY SIR." The rusty voice really did sound contrite. "I HAVE BEEN ORDERED NOT TO ACCEPT ANY FURTHER INSTRUCTIONS FROM YOU."

The Archmage shouldered his way to the front. "I've had enough of this," he said. He stepped out of the lift and stood facing the nearest marine. He held up his staff. "Do you know what this is?" he demanded.

The marine looked him up and down slowly. "Your magic wand won't work here, Tinkerbell," he drawled. "Why don't you get back into the lift, and we'll take you back to your nice cosy cabin?"

The staff was suddenly spinning. The heavy bronze shod foot caught the unfortunate marine in the Y fronts. He doubled over and the staff went into reverse. The other end hit him over the head with a hollow thud. As he began to fall the staff started to spin horizontally. The two marines standing on either side crumpled to the deck simultaneously and only a split second behind their comrade.

A marine moving to attack the old man ran headlong into the staff which the Magician, to his own surprise, was holding straight out in front of him. Another marine lost interest in the proceedings when Betel, whirling like a cross between a dervish and a puppet with cut strings, caught him behind the ear with a lucky kick.

Despite the heroic efforts of the group of friends, the conclusion was never in any doubt. Bryony's arms were held by two squaddies while a third sucked a nasty bite on the forearm he'd stupidly thrown around her from behind. Gloria and Meg were cornered in the lift and threatening jabs with their bronze knives were only delaying their inevitable capture.

The Archmage was pinned to the deck by four burly spacers. The Magician was on his back, his breathing hampered by his own staff - held across his throat by two bruised and very angry opponents. Betel was being dragged bodily across the deck by his ankles, loudly berating his captors.

"Stop!" The voice of the Princess Mrouwl was imperative. "Captain, you will release these people at once, and apologise!"

The Captain smiled a tired smile. "With the greatest of respect, Your Royal Highness," he said, "I must point out that you are exceeding your authority. I would be obliged to obey your instructions if this was a diplomatic affair, but Federation laws have been broken and I have jurisdiction in such matters."

"A diplomatic affair?" purred the Princess. "But this is a diplomatic affair! Now tell your men to release the Ambassador and his people."

"Ambassador?" The Captain was aghast. "What Ambassador?"

"Computer. Please update the Captain on the status of this world."

"THE PRESIDENT OF THE GALACTIC FEDERATION HAS CONFIRMED THAT THE WORLD BELOW US HAS AT LEAST TWO INTELLIGENT LIFE FORMS, ONE OF WHICH IS MOVING TOWARDS CIVILIZATION. HE HAS ALSO CONFIRMED THE APPOINTMENT OF A PERMANENT AMBASSADOR TO REGULATE CONTACT WITH THIS WORLD AND APPRISE THE FEDERATION OF ALL FUTURE DEVELOPMENTS. THIS AMBASSADOR SHALL BE THE MAN KNOWN AS THE MAGICIAN."

The Ambassador, the Archmage and Betel were helped to their feet. Bryony was released and the marines fell back into an honour guard.

"When did this happen?" demanded the shaken Captain.

"EXACTLY FOUR MINUTES AND TWELVE SECONDS AGO."

The Magician shook his head. "The Federation is enormous," he said. "It doesn't move that quickly. Why has it intervened here? And another thing. Why choose me? The President doesn't know me. Come to think of it, I don't even know who the President is."

Mrouwl inclined her head to one side. "Don't you?" she asked. "The President is my father!"

Chapter 27

It was a most unusual wedding. Lord Falcon had insisted on giving Bryony away himself, and had provided an impressive dowry, including spices and fine fabrics from the other side of the planet, beautiful pottery from places almost as far away and precious metals from his own land, wrought with great skill into objects of outstanding beauty. In accordance with local custom, Bryony wore much of the wealth and outshone it all.

Gloria arrived on the arm of the Captain of the *Knight Errant,* resplendent in his full dress uniform. She was a vision of loveliness in white silk and lace, courtesy of the ship's replicator and based on a dress first worn, hundreds of years before, by an imperial princess.

The ceremony, held at the altar of the great stone circle, was led by old Meg and the Archmage, each taking an equal share in the duties and setting an example for future co-operation between their sects.

Betel stumbled through the whole affair in a whirl of wondering amazement. It was without doubt the happiest day of his life, but it would take him a long time to sort the kaleidoscopic memories into any semblance of order. One puzzle, however, had been explained at long last. It had happened near the end of the ceremony, during the exchanging of vows.

"Do you Gloria," asked the Archmage, "take this man to be your husband?"

"I do."

"And do you, Theodore, take this woman to be your wife?"

*The*odore!

Four freshly made beakers were brought and the happy couples tied cords around the moist clay. The twisted string represented the binding together of husband and wife by cords of love and duty – patterns made permanent by the firing of the pots in a kiln. They would keep those beakers all through their lives and would eventually be buried with them, tokens of a bonding that might transcend even the grave.

As darkness fell, Mrouwl came to say goodbye. She left Bryony holding the kitten and made them both promise to look after him.

Later, Gloria and her man stood in the darkness, staring upwards at the star that was carrying their friend back to the Federation. Gloria snuggled closer as she thought how lucky they had been. She was sure that they would be happy here, on this planet that they had adopted. That had adopted them. She stroked his blue hair and mused on the name that Meg had used when speaking of this world.

Earth.

About the author:

Derek Dwyer is a retired schoolteacher. One day he says he'll write down all those outrageous anecdotal stories that every teacher collects in a working lifetime.

His other published works include two activity books in the Ladybird Pirates series, a number of *Practice and Play* books as part of the Ladybird *Read With Me* series in co-operation with Jill Corby and William Murray, a Ladybird National Curriculum Science activity book and a contribution to the Ladybird book *Scary Bedtime Stories*.

He and Merlin Price co-wrote *Warwickshire Jottings*, a book of rural poetry published by Minimax Books (now sadly out of print) and in partnership with Merlin Price he hosts a website at www.pantoscripts.com selling their original scripts to small drama groups all over the world.

www.ingramcontent.com/pod-product-compliance
Ingram Content Group UK Ltd.
Pitfield, Milton Keynes, MK11 3LW, UK
UKHW041941190726
13854UKWH00004B/1730